"GIRL AND HORSE INVOLVED IN BIZARRE
ACCIDENT!"

"HORSE OKAY."

The headlines would shriek these words. Through
a haze of terror I could hear Karen laughing on shore.

"Karen, do something! I can't swim!"

"Don't worry," she said. "The horse can."

Marlon kept moving; farther and farther into the
lake. And I didn't know how to get down off a moving
horse.

The water was up to the stirrups. The heels of my
boots were submerged. Since they were going to get
wet anyway I decided to get off while the getting was
good. The water was up to my waist here, but if I
waited any longer . . .

"Stop, Marlon!" I tugged on the reins.

Marlon didn't stop. The stirrup floated out from
under my left foot. It was too late to get off. Now I
was certain. Marlon *did* mean to go clear across the
lake until he reached the other side. Imagine the surprise of the kids at General Swim when they realize
there's a horse calmly paddling toward them. A horse
with an empty saddle.

HAIL, HAIL CAMP TIMBERWOOD

ELLEN CONFORD

BANTAM BOOKS
TORONTO · NEW YORK · LONDON · SYDNEY · AUCKLAND

To my mother,
who spent some of the most wretched hours
of her life affixing name tags to T-shirts,
and
to my father,
who still maintains I could learn to
swim if I really wanted to.

RL5, II age 11 and up
This low-priced Bantam Book
has been completely reset in a type face
designed for easy reading, and was printed
from new plates. It contains the complete
text of the original hard-cover edition.
NOT ONE WORD HAS BEEN OMITTED.

HAIL, HAIL CAMP TIMBERWOOD
A Bantam Book / published by arrangement with Little, Brown & Company

PRINTING HISTORY
Little, Brown edition published September 1978
Bantam edition/July 1987

Starfire and accompanying logo of a stylized star are registered trademarks
of Bantam Books, Inc. Registered in U.S. Patent and Trademark Office
and elsewhere.

ISBN 0-553-26722-1

Published simultaneously in the United States and Canada

PRINTED IN THE UNITED STATES OF AMERICA

O   0 9 8 7 6 5 4 3 2 1

ONE

Hail, hail to Camp Timberwood,
Nobody likes it, nobody could,
All the counselors carry whips,
The bunks are held up with paper clips.
Hail, hail to Camp Timberwood,
Everyone hates it, everyone should,
If you don't behave all year,
Mommy will send you here.

That's the unofficial Camp Timberwood song. It's sung to the tune of the Notre Dame Fight Song. I learned it by the time we got to camp. It wasn't too hard, considering that a bunch of the old campers must have sung it about fourteen times on the way up. That and "100 Bottles of Beer on the Wall," which, of course, I already knew. We only did that twice though. The bus driver said if we sang it one more time he was going to stop the bus and we could walk the rest of the way to camp. He said it was about seventy-five miles. I would rather have turned around and walked home.

When I first saw the main campus at Timberwood I thought of a giant bowl. All the white, clapboard bunks are arranged around the rim of the bowl and there's a flagpole right in the center of the campus. Then, some distance behind the bunks, there are trees for as far as you can see. The whole area must have been woods before they made a camp out of it.

I was assigned to Bunk 7, the Senior Girls. The inside of our bunk was like a long bedroom, with ten cots, five on each side, lined up against the walls. There were windows, but they had no glass, only screens and canvas shades that rolled down on the outside. The floors were raw planks that looked like they'd give you splinters regularly, and the walls were unfinished pine with exposed beams between the windows. A jail, I thought, must look a lot like this.

We had eight girls and two counselors. Anne Elliot and Joan De Lillo were our counselors. Joanie was only a junior counselor, which meant that she was younger than Anne and sort of her assistant. She was very pretty: long, dark hair and terrific eyes, which she used a lot of eye shadow and stuff on.

In fact, by the time we'd been in camp for six hours Joanie had made up her eyes three times. The first thing she unpacked when we opened our trunks was a small, round mirror that she hung up next to her cot. She was very friendly and bubbly; more like a girl friend than a counselor. I was sure she was very popular with boys.

Anne was pretty too, but kind of cool looking. I don't think she used any makeup at all. Her hair was dark blond and short and she was already tanned, like she'd been in Florida or at the beach since May. She was very tall, and brisk and efficient. But she seemed sympathetic. I was sure I was going to like her.

Our bunk was divided exactly half and half between old and new campers. Audrey Garnet, Reenie Wise, Lou Clarke and Carol Schultz had been to Timberwood before. Erica Stone, Sarah Felton, Diane Turner and me, Melanie Kessler, were new. Sarah had the cot next to mine and I liked her right away. Reenie and Carol seemed nice too. Carol was funny and lively; I thought she was the kind of person who would never be in a bad mood.

About the others it was too soon to tell.

It's a weird feeling to meet nine new people all at once and to know you're going to eat, sleep, shower and do almost everything with them for the next two months. Especially for someone like me. I have no brothers or sisters, so I've always had a room of my own and all the privacy I wanted. And when I don't want privacy, there's always my mother and father.

Maybe that's why I never felt the need for a brother or sister; all my life we've done things together: plays, concerts, Monopoly games, midnight snacks in the kitchen or dinner out at fancy restaurants. We're like three best friends, and this was the first summer that I wouldn't be with them.

My aunt Katherine was to blame for that. They would never have sent me off to camp if she hadn't put the bug into them. Aunt Katherine is a psychiatric social worker and she's the kind of person that no one calls "Kathy" or even "Kate." She is always Katherine. Anyway, she was the one who told them how much good it would do me to get away from them for a while, to be off on my own and have the opportunity to develop some independence and self-reliance.

"She's too dependent on you," Aunt Katherine said. "It's not normal for a thirteen-year-old to be that involved with her parents."

"Maybe it's not normal these days," my father replied, "but I think it's kind of nice. And she's only twelve."

Yay, Daddy, I silently cheered. I heard this whole conversation from my room, where I sat with a book I wasn't reading and the door wide open.

"It's not as if she hasn't any friends," my mother pointed out.

"I know that," said Aunt Katherine, "but she's still an only child who's never been away from her parents. And she'll be thirteen in May. Of course, I can't tell you what to do . . ."

You're certainly trying hard enough, I thought.

"But I think it would be good for all of you if Melanie had at least one summer away. And besides, you don't realize she's going to have *fun*. You sound like I want you to send her to Siberia or something. It's going to be a wonderful experience that she'll remember all her life. I think it's selfish of you not to send her."

Then Aunt Katherine asked them when was the last time they'd spent any time alone together, just the two of them. Didn't they think they deserved a vacation from parenthood for a while?

I leaned forward, listening intently for their answer. But all of a sudden their voices got awfully soft and I couldn't hear what they were saying anymore.

A vacation from parenthood! Why should they want that? We were a *family*. We *loved* each other. Why should you want a vacation from someone you love? *I* certainly didn't need a vacation from *them*.

But Aunt Katherine won. They insisted that she couldn't have talked them into anything that they didn't

4

think would be good for me. No matter how much I protested, their minds were made up. It didn't seem to matter to them what *I* wanted or what *I* thought was good for me. For practically the first time in my life they were pulling rank. They were the Parents, and they knew what was best.

So here I was, in the midst of nine strangers, in a wooden bunk with none of the comforts of home. Instead of dresser drawers we had things called "cubbies" where we were expected to keep all our clothes. Cubbies are like big orange crates set into the wall. As we unpacked Anne said we should roll everything instead of folding it, because it looks neater and takes up less room. Since the cubbies are open, no doors or anything, you can see right into them. I didn't think rolled up sweaters and jeans could possibly take up less space than folded things, but Anne said she'd been a counselor for three years and since I was never a camper before I figured that she ought to know more about things like that than I did.

All the while we were unpacking, Lou and Audrey were talking a mile a minute about kids from last year and making in-jokes about things they knew about Timberwood that none of the new campers understood.

"Lou, do you think Fred is still here?"

"Who's Fred?" asked Erica.

"Oh, Fred," giggled Lou. "Of course he's still here. Who else would take him?"

"Who's Fred?" Erica repeated.

Finally Carol told her that Fred was the handyman. He's like the custodian in school. He's also kind of weird and drinks a lot. Audrey said she was sure that Fred was *watching* her all last summer.

I got a little shiver down my spine. Maybe I ought to mention Fred in my first letter home. *"And by the way, this camp Aunt Katherine made you send me to*

5

has a drunken pervert for a handyman. Maybe Aunt Katherine thinks learning how to avoid drunken perverts who hang around the Senior Girls is good experience for me.''

Then they started talking about what boys were here from last year and if anyone had spotted any cute new ones — but that was mostly Lou and Audrey. They really were boy crazy. They acted like they were years older than the rest of us. They put on this real sophisticated act, even though they were, at the most, one year older than I am.

I was glad I wasn't the only new camper. They could really make a person feel left out.

I listened to their chatter for a while, then started talking to Sarah as we put our "toilet articles" — that's what the camp calls them — in the bathroom cubbies. Sarah was from Bridgeport and she told me that she was at camp on a scholarship.

"I thought that was only for college," I said.

"They have it here too. My parents couldn't afford to send me without some kind of help, so the camp gave them a half-price deal."

"They must have wanted you to come pretty badly to give you a scholarship."

"I don't know. I think they give one or two a year, sort of like a public service. It wasn't that it was me so much. I think maybe they just had the space in this bunk."

Sarah had an air of seriousness about her; not like she was a constant worrier, but just like she looked at life and herself and the things that went on around her as if she was determined to understand the "whys" of everything. She said she liked to draw and paint, and that she had been taking piano lessons since she was seven.

When we went to the mess hall for supper, Carol and Audrey, Reenie and Lou all linked arms and sang "Hail, hail to Camp Timberwood" and marched along in time to it.

Sarah and I walked a little behind them, with Erica and Diane right behind us. It really looked like the division between first- and second-class citizens.

"Boy, is that dumb," Erica sneered. "They act like such show-offs."

I didn't think it was so dumb. It looked kind of warm and friendly and camp-y — the kind of buddy-buddy thing I'd expected camp to be like the few times I thought anything good about it before I arrived. At least, it *would* be warm and friendly if you were one of the people who had her arms linked with the others.

Just then Carol turned around and grabbed my hand. "Come on," she said, "haven't you any camp spirit?"

She crossed her arm over mine and I tugged at Sarah and crossed arms with her on the other side. Carol gave me a big smile as I started to sing along with them. For the first time since getting on the bus I began to feel as if I almost belonged.

I looked sideways at Sarah. She was smiling too.

Then Anne and Joanie, pulling Erica and Diane with them, joined the line on the other side.

"Bunk Seven united!" cried Joanie cheerily.

"A formidable fighting force," proclaimed Anne.

We marched the rest of the way together.

"Now the first meal," Reenie warned us as we sat down around a long table, "is not a true test. The first meal is usually edible. That's so when you write to your parents the first time you don't tell them how really barfo the food is."

The food *was* pretty good. We had chicken and corn and mashed potatoes, with Jell-O for dessert. Lou and Audrey kept poking each other as the waiters went by. Our waiter's name was Ken and he was about sixteen or seventeen. He was kind of fat and looked like he had just gotten a very bad haircut, but that didn't stop Lou and Audrey from giggling and elbowing each other every time he brought something to us.

After supper the whole camp assembled around the flagpole, where Mr. Maxwell, the camp owner ("Call me Uncle Dan"), told us what a wonderful time we would have and some of the activities planned for the week.

He was wearing plaid bermuda shorts and a blue and white Camp Timberwood T-shirt. He said he hoped we would all wear our Camp Timberwood T-shirts as often as possible, because it helped to promote camp spirit.

"And if you need extras, we always have a good supply at the main house," he said. "They're only six dollars apiece."

"I think he makes a profit of three bucks a shirt," Reenie whispered.

Then we all sang the Camp Timberwood Alma Mater—we'd been given mimeographed copies— while the head counselor, Uncle Howie, accompanied us on the accordion.

Camp Timberwood, we'll ne'er forget you,
Even though we're far away,
The friends we make,
Your sparkling lake,
The fun we have all day.
Camp Timberwood, our summer haven,
From you we never want to roam,
The fresh pure air,
And nature everywhere,
Camp Timberwood, our home away from home.

Uncle Dan told us that the alma mater was written by a former camper named Arnold Bing, who became a famous songwriter but who never forgot Camp Timberwood, even though he got rich and successful. I never heard of him, but if that's a sample of the kind of songs he writes, it's no wonder.

I didn't know if I'd ever consider Camp Timberwood my home away from home, but Sarah and I and Anne agreed that there certainly was nature everywhere.

"We hardly have any nature at all in Brooklyn," Anne said.

"Neither do we in Bridgeport," said Sarah. "We can go for days and days without seeing any nature."

Erica looked at us strangely. She has no sense of humor, I decided. I was glad Anne had.

Through this whole rather boring meeting — I guess it was like an assembly in school — Lou and Audrey and Reenie wiggled around and craned their necks, trying to get glimpses of the boys on the other side of the big circle we made around the flagpole.

Lou, I found out later, wears glasses — but doesn't use them, even though she needs them to see any farther than five feet in front of her. So she was squinting up her eyes and nudging Audrey and constantly whispering. "Who's that? Is that Dunc the Skunk? Who's that in the blue shirt? *Is* that a blue shirt? Right next to the fat one — oh, is that a counselor?"

Uncle Dan introduced Aunt Ilene (Mrs. Uncle Dan) who runs the kitchen; she had curly blond hair that I was sure was bleached, and wore big, square sunglasses even though the sun had set. Then, after he pointed out the specialty counselors, like the swimming instructors, the dramatics and arts and crafts counselors, etc., we went back to our bunks.

Bedtime at Timberwood is 9:15! We all agreed

that was downright ridiculous. It's late for the little kids, but none of us goes to bed that early at home. Anne said we'd be glad to get to bed early after a full day of activities, especially since they wake you up at 6:45 A.M! I don't know why camp can't start at nine and end at eleven, or why the older kids don't get to stay up later than the younger ones, but that's the way they do it.

And this is supposed to be a *vacation,* I thought. I never get up earlier than nine or ten o'clock during vacation.

At nine o'clock they played a bugle call over the PA system to warn us that lights out would be in fifteen minutes. And we all had to take turns going to the bathroom, since there were only two sinks, one shower and two toilets for ten people. You had to start getting ready for bed pretty early in order for everyone to be finished by lights out.

They played taps on the PA system, and Joanie hustled the last stragglers out of the bathroom and into bed. Just as the final bugle note sounded, Anne flipped off the light switch.

"Good night. I have to go to a staff meeting, but Joan will be here if you need anything, or get home-sick."

Everyone snickered at that.

"Joan's O.D. for Bunks Six and Seven so she'll be right out on the porch." (O.D. means "On Duty." The O.D. is the counselor in charge at night.)

Boy, was it dark.

I'd had a funny feeling that once I got into bed and had some time to think I was going to feel pretty awful, and I was right. I had a strange, empty feeling in the pit of my stomach; a gnawing, hungry sensation—but not for food. I pictured my room at home, pictured myself snuggling under my soft, downy

10

quilt instead of these two scratchy army blankets. My cot had a thin mattress that sagged under my backside and metal springs that squeaked when I tried to get into a comfortable position. And I missed my clock radio, which I always leave on while I go to sleep.

There were rustling and whispering noises from the other cots and an occasional stifled giggle.

What were my parents doing right this minute? I pictured my father sitting at the dining-room table, staring at my empty chair. My mother sighs. My father pats her arm consolingly. They go into my room and stand over my unslept-in bed. One tear trickles down my father's cheek and he brushes it away angrily.

"Curse your sister Katherine!" he growls. "We should have listened to Melanie."

My mother nods mutely, too emotional to risk speaking. They wander into the living room, where they sit down and stare vacantly off into space, absorbed in guilt and memories of happier summers.

"Mel—are you still awake?"

Sarah leaned over the edge of her cot, half hanging out of it.

"Yeah. Are you?"

"No." She chuckled. Then, soberly, "I feel funny, you know?"

"Me too."

"I think I'm homesick."

"Aren't we kind of old to be homesick?" I asked.

"Well, maybe, but I think I am anyway."

"It's weird. I never get homesick at pajama parties."

"That's different," said Sarah. "You know that's only one night. This is *two whole months*."

There went that feeling in my stomach again. I wished Sarah hadn't mentioned two months. How was I going to endure this awful, aching loneliness for eight weeks, when I didn't even know if I could last through tonight?

"Sarah, what if we feel this way every single night for the whole summer?"

"We won't." She didn't sound very certain though. "I'm sure the first night is the worst. We'll get used to it in a few days."

The bunk was quieting down as people dropped off to sleep. I could hear crickets chirping now. Leaves whispered and rustled and *something* fluttered against the window screens. There were all sorts of strange night noises that I'd never heard in a city apartment.

I was tired, but I still couldn't fall asleep. I tried to picture my parents again. This time, I remembered Aunt Katherine's remarks about a "vacation from parenthood."

My mother and father, in a classy, fabulously expensive nightclub. Their arms entwined, they sip sparkling champagne from crystal-clear stemmed glasses. Between sips, they kiss noisily. They are acting very silly. They gaze at each other lovingly and get up to dance. My mother is wearing a low-cut silver evening dress. My father is in a tuxedo. (Must have rented it.) They dance, cheek-to-cheek, bodies pressed against each other so closely you couldn't get a piece of Saran Wrap between them. They are making out on the dance floor. It is disgusting.

"At last," my father murmurs, "we are alone."

"Mmm," says my mother, snuggling against his neck.

"Two whole months of this—this—divine madness."

"Mmm," says my mother. "But I do hope," she adds dreamily, "that what's-her-name is having a good time at camp."

12

TWO

D*ear Mel,*

We were glad to get your postcard and I hope by this time you have settled down to camp routine and are having lots of fun. You didn't tell us very much in your card, except what you had for dinner the first night, so I hope when you get a chance you'll write us a nice letter with all the details about your activities.

It's very hot here and the air conditioner broke last night, so Daddy suggested we go to a nice, air-conditioned movie. The only one we hadn't seen was an X-rated thing called — well, never mind what it was called. I was so embarrassed I blushed through the whole movie. Your father, on the other hand, laughed uproariously. He thought it was funny. On our way out we ran into three people we know and then I was really embarrassed. Daddy said they must have felt just as sheepish as I did, since they'd gone to the movie too, but that didn't make me feel much better. Thank goodness they're sending someone to fix the air conditioner today!

Your father sends his love and says to write soon and work hard on your swimming.

Love,
Mom

I tossed the letter aside in disgust. Leave them alone for one week and look what happens to their morals. Skulking in and out of X-rated movies, for heaven's sake! And not one word about missing me. Nothing about how lonely the apartment was, or how quiet and dull life had become since I was gone.

If I still had that case of homesickness I'd had the first night, this letter could very well have cured me. My parents were managing very well without me, thank you, and I guess they expected me to follow their example.

Well, to tell the truth, I was managing pretty well. I *had* gotten used to the camp routine and with a couple of exceptions, camp was turning out better than I expected.

Everything runs on charts and schedules and bugle calls at Timberwood. We had to clean up the bunk according to a work chart, which lists jobs everyone has to do in addition to making her own bed. The jobs get rotated every day. Right after clean-up, which is after breakfast, Uncle Howie, the head counselor, comes around and inspects everything. Carol said he might even drop a quarter on your bed to see if it will bounce. (The quarter, not the bed.) You have to pull everything very tight and make hospital corners with all your sheets and blankets. No matter how tight I tucked everything in, I couldn't get a quarter to bounce on my bed. Maybe it's in the way you drop the quarter.

Then there's the activity schedule. It's just like

different periods in school, except it's all supposed to be fun.

Uncle Dan told my parents that there would be two swimming periods a day, one in the morning and one in the afternoon. Once there's swimming instruction and once there's "General Swim" where you just fool around in the water and do whatever you want.

Swimming instruction was one of those exceptions that kept me from completely enjoying myself at Timberwood. My parents were very big on getting me to learn to swim. For years my father had been trying to teach me. Every summer, whether we went to stay in a cottage by a lake, or in a hotel with a pool, or near the ocean, my father would spend two weeks with me in whatever body of water we happened to be near, trying to get me to swim. And every year, the same result. I would spend two weeks in the water with him, never going in any deeper than my chest. There I'd just sort of bob around, flapping my arms and generally avoiding getting my face wet.

Aunt Rosalind, the swimming counselor, insisted that I could not learn to swim if I was afraid to put my head in the water.

"I'm not exactly *afraid*," I told her. "I just don't like to do it."

"Why not?"

"I just don't. It feels — icky — I don't know."

"Don't you want to learn how to swim?"

"Not really," I admitted.

"If you don't learn to swim, you'll be stuck the whole summer in this part of the lake," she warned.

I looked around, following her eyes. We were in the roped-off beginners' area of the lake. I was surrounded by seven-, eight- and nine-year-olds. I towered over everybody but Diane and Sarah.

15

For our first lesson, Aunt Rosalind got us all in a circle holding hands. Sarah was on one side of me and a pale little boy with straggly dark hair and big brown eyes clutched my other hand.

"When I count three, we'll all put our faces in the water and blow bubbles from our mouths, like this." She demonstrated.

"One, two, three!"

Everyone but me and the boy holding my hand put their faces into the water. I just lowered my head and touched my lips to the water and blew out. The little boy squatted down and barely got his chin wet.

"Good work, Tadpoles!" (Tadpoles are what they call the beginners.) "Next time Melanie and Dougie do it too." Aunt Rosalind didn't know everybody's name yet, but she learned mine fast enough.

I sighed impatiently. It didn't seem very sanitary to have everybody sticking their mouths next to everybody else's and germing up the lake like that.

"One, two, three!" I stuck my face into the water, blew bubbles, breathed in and came up choking and sputtering. I had water up my nose and I couldn't stop coughing.

"Your mistake was breathing *in,* Melanie."

Thanks for telling me.

"When our heads are in the water, we only breathe *out.*"

Good rule.

Then we played Ring Around the Rosy. I couldn't believe it. Aunt Rosalind stood there with a straight face and told Diane and Sarah and me we had to play too. When we got to "all fall down" we had to squat down in the water all the way, with our heads beneath the surface.

There was a look of definite panic on Dougie's face when Aunt Rosalind explained the rules of Ring

Around the Rosy. His eyes grew wide and he looked at me pleadingly, as if he expected me somehow to get him out of this. I probably looked as nervous as he did. Who was going to get *me* out of it?

This time I wasn't the only one who wouldn't cooperate. A lot of the little kids wouldn't go all the way in either. I bobbed down just far enough so my mouth was level with the water.

I thought that was progress. At least I got my chin wet.

But Aunt Rosalind wasn't satisfied.

"Melanie, you've been in the water half an hour and your bathing cap isn't even damp. Do you want to be a Tadpole all your life?"

"Aunt Rosalind, some of us aren't cut out to be Sharks and Whales. If it wasn't for us Tadpoles a lot of the big fish would go hungry."

Sarah smiled, but Aunt Rosalind didn't think much of my reasoning.

"I'm sure your parents will be very unhappy if you come home from camp a Tadpole."

I wanted to say they'd be more than unhappy, they'd be shocked, since they were expecting a girl, but I bit my tongue. I didn't mean to be difficult, I just didn't like getting water up my nose and in my ears. It seeps right through the bathing cap and goes "gurgle gurgle squirch."

You have to wear bathing caps for "sanitary reasons." That seems pretty stupid when you consider all the bubbles we blow at each other. What could be more unsanitary than that? But there are a lot of rules at Timberwood that you just don't question. They tell you that all the rules are for our safety and benefit.

One of the rules is that everybody swims twice a day.

Bad rule.

Another exception to my general approval of camp life was Erica Stone. ("Ricky. Nobody calls me Erica.")

She played every game like we were competing in the World Series. At volleyball, which we played against the Junior Girls, she kept screaming, "Spike it, spike it, you retard!" every time I was in the front row. Well, I couldn't spike it every time the ball came to me, because I'm just too short to get it over the net more than once in a while from the front, so I would try to pass it back to someone else.

But she kept on screaming for me to spike it, so after a while, just to stop her screaming, I tried to spike it and nearly got the ball shoved down my throat by a girl on the other team who was about a foot taller than I am, even though she was only eleven.

And the first time we played softball Ricky got a home run every time she was up. I got an accidental single (it wouldn't have been a hit if the pitcher and the second baseman hadn't collided) and that was about it.

Then, when the other team was up I lost a fly ball in the sun and let three runs score. I caught one too, but out there in right field I spent most of the time running after the ball instead of catching it.

"Move your feet, move your feet, get under it, dummy! You want the ball to come to you? Don't stand there like a zombie!"

And Diane repeated everything Ricky said. She followed her around like a pet dog. It was really disgusting. I didn't think I'd ever enjoy softball enough to want to go out there every day and play my heart out, but it certainly was no fun when the two of them yelled through the whole game about how lousy I was.

Nobody else liked Ricky very much except Diane. But she picked on me more than anyone, and maybe it was because of what happened one afternoon on the third day of camp.

We had a basketball game. The court was outdoors, a concrete surface not too far from the softball field. Ricky assigned herself not just to guard her own man, but to guard everybody on the other team, which included me, Lou, Reenie and Sarah. They were killing us — they must have been leading 31 to 6, when Ricky, screeching "I've got it, I've got it!" went up to grab the rebound of one of my many missed shots. She came down with her elbows flying to make sure no one challenged her. *I* wasn't going to challenge her; I was still standing in exactly the same spot from which I had taken the shot, but she plowed into me like a bulldozer and sent me sprawling.

My left hand and the whole side of my left leg were scraped raw against the concrete. When we got back to the bunk, I went into the bathroom to clean my wounds.

"She's so hyper," I grumbled. Reenie, who was standing at the next sink, examined her face in the mirror, looking for spots to dab with her tube of All-Kleer.

"I know," she said.

"She could give Tarzan macho lessons," I went on. "What's she trying to prove?" I bent over, soothing my leg with cold water and a washcloth.

"I'll bet she'd flunk the hormone test at the Olympics," I giggled. "Hey, Reenie, you know how they test all the women to make sure they're really women?"

"Oh hi, Ricky!" said Reenie loudly. I straightened up and turned around. There was Ricky, hands on her hips, glaring at me ferociously.

How much had she heard? I wondered, feeling panicky.

19

Dumb question. One look at the fury in her eyes told me she'd heard enough.

After that, she singled me out for "special attention."

I tried to ignore it, I tried not to show that Ricky's constant hassling got on my nerves, figuring if she didn't get any response she'd stop. But she kept at me, and the more she screamed the tenser I got, and the tenser I got the worse I played, and the worse I played the more she screamed.

Lou and Audrey barely paid any attention to activities at all, let alone to Ricky. If there were no boys around to watch them, their minds were fixed on when the boys *would* be around. They were forever washing their hair or drying their nails or wondering when they were going to be able to wash their hair and how could they put on a catcher's mitt when their nails were still sticky with polish? The last thing on their minds was whatever sport we happened to be playing.

Anne and Joanie tried to get them to participate.

"Lou! Audrey! This is a team sport, girls. Let's all be part of the team! Let's see some of that Bunk Seven fighting spirit!"

They'd look up, act bright and alert for about two minutes, and then go back to whatever they'd been talking about before Anne interrupted them. As for Ricky, they couldn't have cared less what she said to them. They didn't even hear her.

After supper there was evening activity. It would be something different every night, like a movie in the Rec Hall, or a camp fire, with songs and toasting marshmallows, or skits put on by one of the bunks.

When the activity schedule was distributed on Saturday, Carol said, "Hey, look! We have a dance with the Senior Boys tonight!"

Lou and Reenie grabbed at the paper, as if they wouldn't believe the good news unless they read it for themselves.

Audrey dashed into the bathroom yelling, "First in the shower!" and came back clutching a bottle of shampoo, a hairbrush, an eyelash curler and a container of Strawberry Milk Body Lotion.

"Audrey, it's eight-thirty A.M.," Anne pointed out patiently. "You're not going to start getting ready *now*."

"But I have to!" Audrey wailed. "It'll take my hair all day to dry." Audrey's dark blond hair was halfway down her back, and no blow driers are allowed at Timberwood. It's because the electrical system is too weak or something.

Meanwhile, everyone else was yelling out numbers for the shower and before I realized what was happening, only number eight was left.

"Eighth in the shower," I said weakly.

"Nobody goes in that shower until this afternoon," Anne said. "You have a whole day of activities and two swimming periods and you'll just ruin your hair anyway if you do it now."

Audrey grumbled, but Anne was firm.

I'd never been to a dance with boys before. There were a couple in junior high, but I hadn't really felt like going. It was only my first year and I didn't know very many boys. And no one had ever asked me.

How many Senior Boys were there, anyway? There were eight of us girls. What if there were only seven boys? Maybe there were only *six* boys. What if no one asked me to dance? If there weren't enough boys to go around, I might stand there the whole night, alone. It could be awful.

But, I reminded myself, maybe there were ten Senior Boys. Maybe lots of people would ask me to dance. Maybe I wouldn't be able to sit down and catch my breath all evening. Maybe it would actually be *fun*.

Oh, why did they have to give me this to worry about just when everything seemed to be going well? Today I was going to have my first riding lesson, something I'd been looking forward to—maybe the only thing I'd been looking forward to—ever since I knew I had to go to camp.

Now even that was spoiled. All around me the girls were chattering about what they were going to wear while Anne and Joanie, exasperated, tried to prod us through clean-up in time for inspection.

Everybody was excited about the dance. I pushed the broom slowly down the center of the uneven wooden floor, ignoring the hubbub around me.

I wondered what my parents were doing *right this minute*.

THREE

The riding instructor's name was Karen and the lessons were given in a big ring enclosed by a wooden rail. On one side of the ring there was an open field and on the other, a wooded trail down to the lake that you could go on when you got more experienced.

Individual instruction was given three times a week. Not everyone took it, just those people who signed up in advance. You had to pay extra for it.

When I got to the ring for my first lesson, Karen was waiting for me. I took one look at the size of the horse she was standing next to and forgot about the dance completely.

"Okay," she said, "the first thing is how to get on a horse. You always mount a horse from the left side."

"He's awfully big, isn't he?"

"No. He's just your basic horse."

Well, maybe, but I never realized that your basic horse was so *high*. He looked like a nice horse though. He turned his head around to see what we were doing.

"You put your left foot in the stirrup and swing your right foot over the horse's back and into the stirrup on the other side."

"I can't get my leg up that high," I said. The stirrup seemed miles off the ground.

"Grab hold of the saddle."

"I can't reach the saddle!"

"Well, when you get your foot in the stirrup you'll be able to reach it."

I grunted and groaned and raised my foot as high as I could. I even reached down and grabbed my own ankle to try to pull it up higher.

I couldn't reach that stirrup.

"Maybe if I could get a running start," I suggested.

"No, the horse wouldn't like that."

I certainly didn't want to do anything the horse wouldn't like. I patted his side. "Nice horse."

"Well, maybe we can lower it a little," Karen finally relented.

She lowered it maybe an inch.

With a lot of stretching and, at last, an impatient boost from Karen, I mounted the horse. He shifted position a little as I swung into the saddle. I grabbed for the reins.

"Don't pull on the reins!" Karen said.

"But he's moving!" The horse shuffled his feet a little. I was so high up. I felt unsteady, and I needed something to hold on to.

"He won't go any place until you tell him to," said Karen.

"Nice horse. Stand still, horse."

"And he won't rear back and throw you unless you pull the reins too tight."

I dropped the reins like they were on fire. I looked

around for something to clutch, feeling the definite beginning of panic. I was just about to grab the horse's mane when I realized he might not like to have his hair pulled. *I* wouldn't.

"Pick up the reins," Karen directed. "Hold them in both hands, like this." She demonstrated.

"I feel awfully uncomfortable, Karen," I said nervously. "I think this horse is too big for me."

"This is the smallest horse we've got. And the gentlest."

"He won't suddenly decide to run or anything?"

"No. He's very old and he hates to run. Even when he was younger he hated to run. He's a very lazy horse."

"My legs hurt."

"You'll feel a strain in your thigh muscles the first few times. You'll get used to it. Now we're going to walk around the ring for a while."

"On the horse?" I began to panic again.

"Naturally on the horse. You already know how to walk around off the horse." Karen could be sarcastic too. I was glad Ricky wasn't around.

"Kick him gently with your heels, but keep your feet in the stirrups all the time. Pull the left rein a little when you want him to go left and the right rein when you want him to go right."

"How do I make him stop?" That seemed like the most vital piece of information she could give me.

"Pull both reins back, gently."

"He knows all that? He must be a smart horse."

"Come on, Melanie." She knew I was dawdling.

I kicked the horse *very* gently. He didn't move.

"Nice horse," I said, under my breath.

"Kick him a little harder than that, Melanie." Karen sounded sarcastic again.

25

"You told me to kick him gently."

"Yeah, but he has to feel it. The way you did it, he thought it was just a fly."

I kicked him a little harder and pulled the rein to the left. The horse looked up and lazily put one foot in front of the other. I slipped a little in the saddle.

"I'm going to fall off!"

"Don't yell. You won't fall off. Sit up straight and get yourself balanced. Feet in the stirrups."

Very slowly, like a tired old man, the horse began to walk around the ring.

I kept my knees tight against him, like Karen told me, and my back as straight as I could. When the horse got back to where we had started, he stopped, without my even pulling on the reins.

"Nice horse," I said gratefully. "Smart, good horse."

"Don't talk to the horse," Karen warned. "It distracts him."

Just as she said that he turned his head around to try to look at me, poked his nose at my hand and whinnied.

I shrieked again.

"Stop yelling, Melanie, You'll make him nervous."

"He's making *me* nervous."

"And keep your hands back."

After a couple of more walks around the ring I felt much more at home on the horse. He didn't try to break into a run once, though it must have been very boring for him just circling that ring over and over again. He seemed very patient, but I could swear he sighed a couple of times.

For my first lesson I thought I did pretty well. At least I didn't fall off and I didn't make the horse rear back and throw me. I felt less and less nervous as I got used to being up so high and once I realized that a little slipping in the saddle didn't necessarily mean I'd fall on my head and crack my skull, I was much more relaxed.

Karen wanted to start me on trotting, so I must have done pretty well. Only, the period was practically over, so I said it might be better if we waited until the next time to start something new.

I figured there was no point in pressing my luck.

It was a fairly long walk from the riding area to my bunk and as I started back I realized that I hadn't thought about the dance once through the whole lesson. But now it all came back in a rush, the nervousness, the anxiety about being left out; imagine what fun Ricky would have with me if I were the only girl not dancing.

"Hey, Melanie, maybe you've got bad breath."

"Why don't you use some of this perfume, Melanie? Maybe that'll help. It's called 'Wallflower.' "

I brushed these thoughts away impatiently. It was just as likely that no one would ask *Ricky* to dance. After all, she was so nasty that even boys who didn't know her would be able to see right away what kind of a person she was. And if *she* didn't dance the whole night either, she could hardly make fun of *me*.

I crossed the field and passed the Arts and Crafts shack. Behind it was a clump of birch trees and an enormous rock. Sitting on the rock, looking down at his feet, was Dougie Tepper, the little boy from my swimming group.

I started to walk by him, but the way he looked, sitting there all alone on that big rock, his head slumping and his hands lying limply in his lap, got to me.

"Hey, Dougie."

"Hi, Melanie."

27

"What are you doing here all alone? Where's the rest of your group?"

"In there." He pointed toward the shack.

"Why aren't you in there too?"

"I didn't want to make a lanyard. So Joel said if I didn't want to do what everyone else was doing I didn't have to. So I came out here."

I squatted down next to him. "How come you didn't want to make a lanyard?"

"Because I can't. And Celia kept showing me how but I still couldn't get those plastic things crossed the right way and everyone laughed at me. They said I was stupid."

Celia is the Arts and Crafts counselor.

"That's silly," I said firmly. "You're not stupid. Sometimes it just takes a while to catch on. Look how much trouble I'm having learning to swim and I'm not stupid."

"Yeah, me too." He began to poke at a scab on his knee. He swung his feet back and forth so his heels smacked against the edge of the rock.

"So what are you going to do?" I asked. I hated to leave him there. He looked so miserable.

"Wait for my brother. Maybe he'll talk to Joel and I won't have to do Arts and Crafts anymore."

"Your brother? Who's your brother?"

"Steve. He's in Bunk Eight."

That was the Senior Boys' bunk.

"Does he know you're waiting here for him?"

"No. And he'll probably be mad. He says I'm a big baby. But I don't care. He's always mad at me anyway. He thinks I'm a pest."

"Doesn't sound like a very nice brother," I muttered.

"I don't care. As long as he fixes it so I don't have to do Arts and Crafts."

28

"Look, I'm going to see your brother tonight," I said.

"You are? You know Steve?"

"Not yet, but I will," I promised. "And I'll talk to him for you, okay? Because you could wait here all day and he might not come along."

Dougie looked up at me, his face bright with hope.

"And you'll tell him about letting me not do Arts and Crafts?"

"Sure." I'll also tell him what I think of him for being so rotten to his own brother. A poor little kid like this needed help, not insults.

"How about going back inside now?" I suggested. "You could say you'd like to just watch them make lanyards."

"They'll laugh at me again. No one will let me watch them."

His gloom returned.

It was a shame that he was out here all alone. I could understand how he felt. Why should I urge him to go back to the Arts and Crafts shack, just so all the other kids could make fun of him and pick on him? If he was happier out here alone on his rock, I didn't blame him.

"Okay. But I have to go now."

"You won't forget to talk to my brother?"

"I won't forget," I promised. "See you in swimming."

I walked off without looking back, but I was sure I could feel his eyes following me, all the way down to the rim of trees that surrounded the main campus.

Now I couldn't wait for the dance. While everyone else in the bunk might be thinking of romance and moonlight and boy friends and silly, unimportant things like that, I had a vital mission to accomplish.

I would find this Steve and teach him a thing or

29

two about kindness to his fellowman. Or fellow-brother. Or whatever.

I felt positively noble as I strode back to the bunk. I held my head high and tried to ignore the awful charley horse that was beginning to stiffen my thighs into two oak planks.

But by the time I got halfway across campus my proud stride had become a pitiful hobble.

FOUR

As I staggered into the bunk and limped past Ricky's cot, which was closest to the door, I was greeted with a loud, retching noise.

"Hey, Mel, you *smell!*" she roared.

Ignoring her, I sank down on my own cot and began tugging off the brand-new, extremely expensive riding boots that my mother had bought me, and that I had insisted fit perfectly. They didn't feel so perfect now, but neither did the rest of me.

"Listen, forget whose turn it is in the shower," Ricky said. "Let Mel go first. For the good of the bunk."

"Yeah," said Diane, "I'll give up my turn. You go now, Melanie. For the good of the bunk."

Little Ms. Echo. I yanked off the other boot and groaned.

"Charley horse?" asked Carol sympathetically.

"Yeah. I never realized what a good name that is. Charley *horse.*"

"What you need," said Joanie, "is a nice, hot bath. Unfortunately, we don't have a bathtub . . .''

31

"So you can take a shower instead," finished Ricky. "Come on, Mel, do us all a favor and take your shower now. Diane's letting you have her turn."

"Yeah, you can have my turn," persisted Diane.

"Is there an echo in here?" I asked Joanie. She grinned.

"Well, if Diane's letting you have her turn," she said.

"There *is* an echo in here," I muttered.

"Why look a gift horse in the mouth?" Joan asked.

"Gift horse," I mumbled. "Very cute. *Gift horse.*"

I hauled myself off the bed and collected clean clothes from my cubby.

Anne was in the bathroom washing out something in the sink and shouting to Audrey in the shower.

"No you can't," she called. "You knew you couldn't use a blow drier here. You shouldn't have brought it."

"But they have good outlets up at the main house!" Audrey wailed. (The main house is where Uncle Dan, Aunt Ilene and the specialty counselors live.) "It would only take me ten minutes—"

"Then I'd have to let everybody do it or it wouldn't be fair. Aunt Ilene would have a fit."

"Oh, Anne!" whined Audrey.

"Oh, Audrey!" replied Anne, in exactly the same whine. "Hurry out of that shower. You're holding everyone up."

Audrey emerged, dripping, from the shower. "If you'd let me do my hair before it would've been dry by now," she grumbled. Muttering, she briskly rubbed herself down with a towel.

"I'm sorry," Anne said, "but you can't skip a whole day's activities while you wait for your hair to dry."

Audrey stalked out, leaving a cloud of talcum powder hanging in the air behind her.

I stripped down to my underwear, stepping gingerly out of my jeans. The way everyone ran around the bunk in various stages of undress, it hadn't taken me more than a couple of days to lose my shyness about getting in and out of clothes in front of other people. And so far, at least, no one had seen Fred anywhere around. (Reenie decided that he had either been fired, or had drunk himself to death.)

"A little sore?" asked Anne, watching me.

"A lot sore," I groaned.

The hot shower felt great — while I was in it. While the water ran down my body I pictured it washing away all the aches and pains.

But when I got out of the shower and dried myself off, I didn't feel one bit less stiff than I had before.

Lou looked up from painting her toenails and "tsked" as she watched me drag myself out of the bathroom.

"You're not going to be able to do much dancing tonight," she said.

I flopped down on my cot. "I'm not sure I'll even be able to walk to the mess hall."

Not that I was concerned about it anymore, since, even if I was able to dance, that wasn't what I was looking forward to. But Lou assured everyone that there would be plenty of boys to choose from. If there was a shortage of Senior Boys, the waiters filled in. Lou smiled dreamily at the prospect of all those older guys.

When we got to the canteen after supper, Carol and Sarah practically had to carry me up the steps. A cluster of boys near a phonograph observed our ungraceful entrance.

"Is she drunk or what?" asked one of them. I recognized him as the boy Lou called "Dunc the Skunk." His real name was Duncan Schenk.

"Dunc the Skunk!" shrieked Lou, racing over to him as if she hadn't seen him for a year. Actually, she'd seen him barely an hour ago outside the mess hall.

"Horseback riding," explained Carol. "Melanie had her first riding lesson today."

"Aww," said Dunc. "Poor thing." He yanked out a chair. "Sit down, sit down. You can sit, can't you?"

I smiled bravely. "That's about all I *can* do." I sat. I realized that I was surrounded by boys. Carol, Lou and Sarah were standing next to us, but I was sitting right in front of the record player and four boys were gathered around it, selecting records. I looked up at the unfamiliar faces, wondering if one of them was Dougie's brother.

"You can help us pick out records, Melanie," said another boy. "Can't you dance at all?"

"I'm not sure. Right now sitting seems to be my best thing."

Lou and Audrey kind of elbowed their way in so they were in the center of the group of boys with me.

"Do they still have the same great records as last year?" asked Lou.

"Oh, yeah," said Duncan. "Exactly the same. Al Jolson singing 'Swanee.' 'Stephen Foster Favorites.' 'A Million and One Strings Play Bach's Biggest Hits.' "

"You're kidding," I giggled.

A slim, brown-haired boy looked down at me with a fake sorrowful expression.

"He's not kidding. And we have to be real careful with them, because these records are actual antiques."

34

"Steve!" yelled Lou, "Steve Tepper! I didn't even recognize you!"

"Hi, Lou."

"You look so *different*. Doesn't he look different, Aud?"

Aud stared. "He really does."

Steve Tepper. Dougie's brother. My project for the evening. I didn't know how he looked last year, but right now he looked terrific. He was a few inches taller than me and had nice, smooth skin and terribly intelligent brown eyes.

"All week I kept wondering who that new guy was and it turns out to be an old guy," Lou marveled.

By this time virtually everyone was crowded around the phonograph and Lou said, "Put something on."

"Did you bring your records, Lou?" asked Duncan.

"I couldn't," she moaned tragically. "I tried, but we just couldn't fit them into my trunk. My mother said she'd mail them but they haven't come yet."

I looked down at the albums in front of me.

" 'The Harmonicats Play Rodgers and Hart'?" I asked incredulously. " 'The Magic Accordion of Pete Boroni'? 'Midnight in Minsk'?"

I glanced up questioningly at Steve.

He was just about to say something when Ricky practically bulldozed her way into the center of the group and pushed herself right up against him.

"I thought this was supposed to be a dance," she complained. "How come nobody's dancing?"

"Well, put something on," Audrey said impatiently.

" 'Polkas You Know and Love'?" I suggested. " 'Memorable Marches of the Civil War'?" Steve grinned wickedly. Ricky narrowed her eyes and looked from me to Steve and back again.

She moved even closer to him, if that was possible.

Audrey grabbed an album called "Swing and Sway with Leon Newhouse."

"Put this one on."

"Ah, an old favorite," said Dunc. He put it on and turned the volume way up. "Anybody here know the rhumba?" he yelled.

Steve leaned over and started to ask me something.

"Oh, poor Mel can't dance," interrupted Ricky. "She's so charley-horsed she can hardly move." She actually yanked Steve's arm and pulled him to the center of the canteen.

The crowd around me dissolved as people found partners and began to dance to the sticky strains of Leon Newhouse's Society Orchestra.

Before I even had time to reflect on how handsome Steve was, and on how maybe I ought to think twice about the lecture on Brotherhood that I'd planned to give him, a boy perched on the table next to the record player and said, "I appointed myself in charge of keeping you from being lonely."

He was short and blond with blue eyes that could only be described as twinkly.

"Thanks," I said. "That's very nice. I'm Melanie Kessler."

"I'm Jay Overgaard. Are you really temporarily crippled?"

We had to shout over Leon Newhouse.

"I'm not sure. I have been all afternoon."

"You want to try and dance? The only thing I can do is the box step and the way I do it you practically stay in the same spot through the whole dance, so it wouldn't put too much of a strain on you."

"Okay, I can try." I stood up slowly. "Ouch," I said, trying to make it sound like a joke. My thighs still ached. In fact, they felt stiffer than ever.

"A little exercise might do you good," Jay advised. He put his arm around my waist and took my hand.

"Yeah, as little as possible," I agreed.

He was right though about the way he danced; it didn't strain me at all. He really did do only the box step, so we simply traveled in a teensy square, front, right, back, left, over and over again.

Audrey passed us, dancing with Ken, our waiter, who was not that much better a dancer than Jay, but who covered more territory. Steve and Ricky danced by. Ricky had her cheek pressed against Steve's shoulder, both eyes closed and a dreamy expression on her face. It looked phony.

"I thought you couldn't dance!" Steve called as they went by. Ricky's eyes snapped open.

"I thought so too," I said.

When the number was over, Jay led me back to my chair near the phonograph. "You know, my parents paid a dancing school twenty-five dollars to teach me that?"

"Really? Well, I'm glad," I said. "I enjoyed it very much." That was the truth. Jay didn't know it — nobody knew it except me — but this was the first time in my life that I had ever danced with a boy.

And I liked it.

Before I had a chance to sit down, Steve was at my side. Without Ricky.

"Now that you can dance," he said.

"Nothing strenuous, Steve," Jay warned. "She's in a very delicate condition."

"I don't think there's anything strenuous you can do to the music of Leon Newhouse," Steve assured him. "I'll treat her like a — a — fragile sculpture."

A fragile sculpture! I sighed as Steve put his arm around my waist. That was the most romantic thing

I'd ever heard. He pulled me closer to him and I felt an unfamiliar flutter in my chest.

I rested my cheek against his shoulder like Ricky had. I wondered if he could feel my heart thumping. After all, it was practically right against his.

"Amazing recovery you made, Melanie." Ricky's sarcastic voice shattered the lovely moment.

As we danced by where she was box-stepping with Jay, she wrinkled up her nose.

Did I still smell of horse? I felt a flash of panic. Was I, at this very moment, turning Steve off by smelling like a *stable?*

As quietly as I could, I sniffed. Twice. Three times.

There wasn't a trace of horse. All I could smell was my own Green Apple cologne and a nice, clean, soapy smell that I realized was Steve.

I sighed contentedly and forgot about Ricky

The canteen is equipped with tables, chairs and soda machines. I guess it's supposed to look like an old-fashioned "Sweet Shoppe" where the kids used to go after school in the old days, or in the movies. For the dance, all the tables and chairs were pushed against the walls and between dances you could rest with a Coke and catch your breath.

After a couple of dances with Steve he sat me down at one of the tables and strolled over to the machine to get me a Coke. I watched him as he walked; he was just the right height for me and his white jeans fit him so nicely. A lot of boys I knew at home didn't look very together in what they wore, but Steve seemed to me to be perfectly beautiful in his clothes.

Not only that, he was so much more *mature* than any of the boys I knew from school. He didn't talk very much when we were dancing, but that might be because he was sure enough about himself not to have to say any silly thing that came into his head just to keep a conversation going.

A lot of boys my age in school act so babyish when they're around girls that they make me feel years older than them. But Steve was different. He told me he was going into his first year of high school, so maybe that was the reason, but he seemed a lot older than the one-and-a-half-year difference between us.

In fact, I began to worry that I might start acting like some of those boys in school and say something so dumb that Steve would think I was absolutely *juvenile* and go looking for someone sophisticated, like Lou, so I hardly said anything at all either.

Maybe when you were comfortable with someone, no words were necessary, I thought dreamily. Maybe you just *knew*, without spelling it out, that you were *meant* for each other.

I guess I just sat there with a totally dopey expression on my face, because I heard Sarah say, "Hey, Mel, having fun?" before I even realized she was standing right in front of me.

"Oh, yeah." I almost giggled. *"Yeah."*

"Feeling better?"

"Better and better."

I grinned at her and she nearly burst out laughing. "Me too," she said, "if you're interested."

"I'm interested!" I felt suddenly guilty that I hadn't even looked to see who she'd been dancing with.

"I think Alan likes me," she said shyly. "I danced with him three times already."

"Which one is Alan?"

"Over there." She pointed to the Coke machine. Standing next to Steve was a stocky boy with jeans and a Beethoven T-shirt. He had long, nearly black hair, dark skin and was nowhere near as beautiful as Steve.

"Oh."

"He's very nice," said Sarah. "He plays the violin."

"Well, that's perfect," I said brightly. "You two should make beautiful music together."

Sarah kind of drifted away as Steve returned with the Cokes. He handed me one and was just about to sit down next to me when Ricky appeared out of nowhere and planted herself at his right elbow.

"Gee that looks good," she said sweetly, eyeing my Coke. "Do you think you could get me one, Steve?"

He looked at me for a second, almost apologetically, then handed her his Coke. "Here, take mine. I'll share Melanie's. You don't mind, do you, Mel?"

"Not a bit," I purred.

I remembered a scene from this incredibly sad old Bette Davis movie, where her lover lights two cigarettes all the time and gives her one. I passed the Coke over to Steve and watched him take a swig. When he handed it back to me I took a big gulp from the bottle without wiping the rim. We were just like the lovers in that movie. I couldn't resist flashing Ricky a superior smile.

She guzzled her Coke, perched on the edge of our table. I could almost see the wheels turning in her head as she tried to figure out what move to make next.

I could even feel a bit of pity for her. It was kind of pathetic, actually, the way she was so desperately throwing herself at Steve.

"Let me see your palm," she said suddenly.

Steve looked at her blankly for a moment. As he hesitated, she took his hand and held it in hers.

"Mmm," she said, "very interesting."

She began to trace lines on his palm with her fingers, very gently. I clenched my teeth.

"Do you read palms?" asked Steve.

40

"Mmm hmm," she murmured, gazing down at his. He bent his head next to hers, eager to see what she was discovering.

I seethed inside. I couldn't stand it, watching her mess around with *my* Steve's hand.

"Want some Coke?" I asked. I held out the bottle to him.

"Thanks," he replied absently. He took a drink and thrust the bottle back in my direction without even looking at me.

"What do you see?" he asked.

I never found out, because just then Duncan came by and asked me to dance.

"Gladly," I said, which is not easy to say with your teeth clenched.

I tried to keep an eye on them while I danced with Duncan. As soon as Duncan let me go, Jay returned and we box-stepped through an accordion rendition of "Funiculi Funicula." I thought I saw Steve look around for me as Jay and I started to mark out our little square of the dance floor, but after a quick glance in my direction he took Ricky's hand and danced with her.

"Last dance!" announced Anne, who had been quietly supervising from a corner of the canteen, along with Harvey, the Senior Boys' counselor.

Jay was still clutching my hand as I craned my neck around to find Steve.

But Duncan descended upon us and took my hand from Jay's.

"Do you mind?" he asked Jay. "They're playing *our* song."

Frustrated because I didn't see Steve, when this was the last chance I'd have to be with him, I let Duncan adjust us into dancing position.

"What's our song?" I asked distractedly.

"Anything by Leon Newhouse."

There he was! And Ricky was snuggled up against his shoulder again with that revolting, gooey expression on her face, swaying to "I'll See You in My Dreams."

Duncan hummed loudly along with the male singer on the record and clutched me closer to him. Even though my chin only came up to his chest, his shaving lotion was like an attack on my nostrils. I couldn't imagine why he needed shaving lotion. I pulled back. He unclutched a little.

The dance was over.

"I'll walk you back to the bunk," Duncan announced.

"Are you allowed?"

"Sure. But if we're not back in ten minutes Harvey'll come after us."

Why couldn't it be Steve walking me back to the bunk? Where *was* he? Everyone was leaving the canteen now, some of the boys alone, some with girls.

Sarah and Alan were right ahead of us. Duncan helped me down the steps. I hadn't even thought about my charley horse for an hour but now, suddenly, it hurt again. Or at least, I remembered that it hurt.

Then I saw Steve. He was alone, hands stuck in the pockets of his crisp, white jeans. He walked toward Bunk 8. I wanted to call out to him, to yell that this was a big mistake, my getting stuck with Dunc the Skunk, that I never wanted anything in my life so much as to have Steve walk me back to my bunk.

But Duncan had his arm around my shoulders and was firmly steering me in the direction of Bunk 7, and I knew it would be very uncool to knock Duncan's arm away and go tearing across campus after Steve, yelling all those things I was thinking.

Joan stood on the front steps as we got back, keeping a sharp eye on returning couples.

"Well, good night, Duncan," I sighed.

"Good night. I hope you aren't crippled much longer."

"Oh, I feel better already. I guess the exercise did me good."

He started to bend down and I suddenly realized he was about to kiss me. I also realized I did not want him to kiss me. I stepped back quickly, leaving him standing there with his head bent over and his chin stuck out, looking as if he might topple forward in a moment. Hastily he straightened up, looked around and cleared his throat.

" 'Night," I said.

Diane and Ricky were in a huddle on Ricky's cot when I walked in. Diane snickered as I passed them. Ricky narrowed her eyes and gave me the nastiest little smile.

Reenie was lying on her cot with her hands behind her head and crisscrossing her legs in the air. At the same time she sang, "I dream of Reenie with the light bro-own hair," and giggled at regular intervals.

I flopped down on my cot. Sarah wasn't back yet. Carol flung the screen door open and bounded in. She took one look at Reenie and said, "Aww, poor Reenie. Didn't you have a good time?"

That broke them both up. Reenie's legs came thumping down and she jumped off the cot and practically skipped over to her cubby to get her pajamas.

"Must be nice to have two strong legs," I muttered.

"Ohh, I forgot about your poor legs," said Reenie soberly. "Aren't they any better?"

"Oh, that's okay." I felt foolish. It really wasn't her healthy legs I envied, it was her high spirits. "I was even able to dance."

"I noticed, I noticed," she said, flinging things

wildly about in her cubby. "Dunc the Skunk couldn't take his eyes off you."

"Yeah."

"Not to mention Steve," said Carol. "Didn't he get cute in just a year?" she asked Reenie.

Diane and Ricky were hanging on every word.

"Oh, well, he's okay, but did you see *Gene?* You know, all night he kept singing 'I dream of Reenie with the light brown hair'? No matter what music was on he kept singing that. Isn't that cute? So then I started singing 'I dream of Genie with the dark brown hair,' which is awfully appropriate, and then I started thinking about how cute Reenie and Gene sounds. Or Gene and Reenie. Don't you think that sounds cute?"

"Adorable," said Carol. Their voices faded as they disappeared into the bathroom.

Sarah, Lou and Audrey came in, shooed by Anne and Joanie.

Sarah sat down on her cot and smiled at me.

"Nice time?" I asked.

She nodded.

It took a while before everyone settled down and Anne got the lights out. Even after she and Joan left and the O.D. came on, the whispering and giggling continued. The O.D., a counselor named Marcia, kept pleading with us to "keep it down to a dull roar, girls," but that didn't do much good.

I lay on my cot, blankets pulled up to my chin, feeling . . . cheated. Why had Steve seemed to like me and then fallen for Ricky's phony act? Couldn't he see what kind of a person she really was? And why did Ricky have to come barging in at all, ruining everything for me? Wasn't she satisfied with picking on me and ridiculing me during the day without stealing my boy friend too?

My boy friend? Well, he might have been. If it

44

weren't for *her*. Sure, Duncan liked me and I figured Jay was interested too, and it was flattering and all that. Especially after worrying about being a wallflower and having no boy even look at me, it was kind of a nice feeling to know that there were two boys who would probably be glad to go with me if I just said the word.

But I didn't want either of them. When I danced with Jay my pulse didn't do weird, fluttery things. When Duncan wanted to kiss me my first impulse was to jump away. It was Steve I wanted. Steve, who seemed to forget me even faster than he got to know me. Why I felt this way I didn't know. I just knew that if it had been Steve bending down to kiss me, instead of Duncan, I wouldn't have jumped away.

Like a sneak attack came a stab of homesickness. I wish the summer was over, I thought. I wish I was home, rid of all these problems I never had before. I wish I could see my mother.

Just before I fell asleep I remembered that I had never kept my promise to Dougie.

FIVE

Sarah and I stood waist deep in the part of the lake roped off for beginners. It was General Swim, where we didn't have to do anything except have a good time. I found it impossible to have a good time in the water, especially since Ricky and Diane, who was already a Sunfish and allowed into the deeper water, spent a good part of the time making snide remarks about Tadpoles. Ricky splashed past us doing a disgustingly professional backstroke. Diane, swimming overhand behind her, stopped to pass the time of day.

"Did you put your face in the water yet, Melanie?"

"Ignore her," advised Sarah.

"If I was in with the babies," said Diane, "I probably wouldn't want to put my face in the water either. You know what *they* do in the lake."

"You used to *be* one of the babies, Diane," I pointed out. "I guess that's how you know what babies do in a lake."

She scowled and swam away.

"She's weird," commented Sarah, watching Diane follow Ricky around. "She really *is* a baby."

Dougie, yanking his "buddy" along, waded up to us. (In General Swim you have to have a buddy. Whenever the waterfront counselor blows a whistle, you grab your buddy's hand and hold it up. Then, if a counselor spots a person without a buddy, the counselor knows that someone has probably drowned. They blow the whistle every few minutes, but even so, I figure that by the time they realize a buddy is missing it's probably too late.)

"You won't forget tonight, will you, Melanie?" Dougie had asked me this about ten times already. He was bitterly disappointed when I told him that I hadn't had a chance to talk to Steve about Arts and Crafts. I felt guilty. I knew I had really let him down.

"Dougie, if I get a chance to see him, I'll definitely talk to him. I *promise*."

And I meant it. What difference did it make now anyway if I dumped on Steve for being mean to his brother? It wouldn't change anything between us because there wasn't anything between us to change. It was probably just as well. A boy who was that mean to his own brother was probably not a very nice boy anyhow.

He'd certainly seemed nice though. Extremely nice.

"He's just right for you, Melanie!" Ricky yelled. She pointed to Dougie. "You make a lovely couple. A couple of *what*, I don't know—"

Dougie looked confused. I stalked through the water, trying to walk fast but not able to build up much speed, till I reached the other side of the beginners' section.

Sarah, Dougie and his buddy followed me.

"Let's practice the face float," suggested Sarah. "I'm getting sick of being stuck here."

"Why? You want to be out there with *them?*"

We were working on the face float and the back float in lessons but I wasn't doing too well. I liked the back float as long as I didn't sag in the middle and drop under the water, but I could really live without ever doing a face float.

"Listen, Sarah, they also call the face float the dead man's float. There has to be a reason for that."

"Come on, Mel, let's practice."

"You know why they call it the dead man's float, don't you, Sarah?"

"I'll do it if you do, Melanie," said Dougie. He looked very brave. Since he was having as much trouble learning to swim as I was, I thought that *was* very brave of him.

"I'll do it if you do it, Doug," said his buddy.

What a responsibility. I sighed. If I would just practice the face float with Sarah, both these little kids might get over their fear and actually learn to swim. I could probably change their whole lives if I would simply put my face in the water and float. Maybe the other kids would even stop picking on Dougie and he would get some self-confidence and . . .

Sarah was already prone in the water, arms stretched in front of her.

"Hey, Melanie," came Ricky's voice, "why don't you practice drowning?"

That did it.

I took a deep breath, flung myself down into the water and did a perfect face float. I stayed there as long as I could, holding my breath. Then I scrambled to my feet, shaking the water out of my eyes and nose.

"Hey, that was great," said Sarah.

"Yeah," I gasped, feeling rather proud of myself. "It wasn't bad. Now you, Dougie."

48

He bit his lip. He inhaled very dramatically, bent his knees and sort of fell into the water. Almost immediately he jumped up and exhaled loudly, as if he'd been holding his breath for ten minutes.

"Very good, Dougie!" Sarah applauded.

Dougie turned to his friend. "Now you, Jason."

"You weren't hardly down at all," Jason said.

"You said you'd do it if I did!" Dougie cried. "You *said!*" He turned to me, outraged. "Didn't he say he would, Melanie?"

Jason shrugged, trying to look as if it didn't matter to him one way or the other.

"Oh, all right." Not even giving himself a moment to take a deep breath or to think twice about what he was going to try, he hurled himself forward, like Superman taking off from a tall building in a single bound, and splashed in face down. It wasn't graceful, but he did it.

"Yay!" I yelled.

He stood up, coughing. "See," he said, between gasps, "I can do it."

"Now let's all do it together," Sarah said. "Side by side."

"Um, don't you think we're overdoing this a bit?" I asked. "These little ones may have had enough for one day."

"That's touching, Mel," she said, with a sarcastic grin. "The way you worry about their welfare. No, I don't think we're overdoing it. The sooner you stop being a Tadpole, the sooner Ricky has one less thing to hold over your head."

Good point.

Sarah counted to three and we all floated. Then Sarah made us see who could float the longest. The last one to stand up won. By the time General Swim ended I was positively waterlogged.

49

"I think I drank half the lake," I said as we walked back to the bunk. "Burp."

"It was worth it," said Sarah. "Do you realize if we show Aunt Rosalind we can do the face float and the back float and blow bubbles we'll be Frogs by the next lesson?"

"Ribbit," I replied.

Dear Mom and Dad,

By the time you get this letter I may be a Frog. That's the step higher than Tadpole in swimming. I also did very well at my riding lesson.

We had a dance with the Senior Boys. I met a boy I like but I think he likes somebody else, even though he seemed to like me at first. [I crossed out everything after "Senior Boys."]

I miss you a lot. I still get homesick sometimes. You seem to be okay though. I'm glad you're not missing me too much. [I really wasn't glad at all, but I couldn't say that I wished they were suffering.]

The food is not as good as I thought, but it's not horrible. We're going to have a movie tonight. Walt Disney I think. No X-rated movies here, ha ha.

Love,
Mel

By the time I finished my letter the bugle call had sounded and we had to go for supper. I took the letter with me to drop in the basket they keep outside the mess hall. You had to write home three times a week, even if it was only a postcard, to let your parents know you hadn't been bitten by a snake or drowned. Uncle Howie stood by the basket on letter days and made sure no one got into the mess hall without dropping something in the basket first.

I had to plow through a crowd of people around the mail basket. They were all tossing letters into it and yelling to Uncle Howie to make sure he saw them.

I held up my letter and waved it toward him. "See, I'm putting a letter in. Okay?"

He nodded, looking a little frantic.

I turned around to squirm out of the mob and found myself face to face with Steve.

I closed my eyes for a second and swallowed hard. When I opened them he was still there, looking down at my face, studying me. I couldn't move. I was blocking the route to the mail basket. Elbows were being jammed in my ribs and my back and people were shoving me every which way and I hardly felt any of it.

"Hi," he said.

"Hi."

This is ridiculous, I told myself. I'm only thirteen. I'm too young to be in love with anyone. So why is my heart thudding down into my stomach like that? Why do I suddenly feel as if the breath had been knocked out of me?

"How's your charley horse?"

"Oh. Better. Thanks."

He had on a blue and white checked shirt and jeans. He reached past me and dropped a postcard into the basket. He didn't even bother to check that Uncle Howie saw him. That's class, I thought.

And then, why do his clothes fit him so perfectly? Why can't he look a little tacky? Why am I standing here in the middle of this crush of people thinking these dumb things?

"Come on," he said. He put his hand on my shoulder and led me out of the mob scene. I don't know how we escaped, because when I felt his hand on my shoulder I closed my eyes and concentrated on not melting.

Why had I written a letter to my parents instead of washing my hair after swimming?

Why was I wearing my ratty old Gemini T-shirt?

Why did his clothes fit him better than mine fit me?

We went into the mess hall. His hand was still on my shoulder. It didn't *have* to be. I knew how to get into the mess hall from in front of the mess hall. I wouldn't have gotten lost. We were no longer in the midst of a sea of elbows; what was he protecting me from?

Everybody saw us. Most of the Senior Boys were already at their table, which was right next to the entrance. Everyone could see Steve's hand on my shoulder. Diane pushed past us, turned around and did a slow stare. I ignored her. I looked up at Steve, question marks in my eyes.

"Save me a seat at the movies," he said.

He dropped his hand from my shoulder and went to sit down.

I just stood there for a moment. I was half aware that Duncan's eyes were on me and that although there was an empty spot right next to him at the table, Steve went around to the other side and took a seat on the far end of the bench from him.

I walked slowly to my own table near the back door of the mess hall. I didn't understand anything, and I wasn't thinking straight enough to figure it out. At the dance, Steve had seemed to like me at first but then — He didn't even look for me after he met Ricky. He'd let Duncan walk me back to the bunk.

Yet today —

Did he see me today and realize that he was madly in love with me after all? How come I was suddenly so irresistible? Or had he liked me all along, but thought I liked Duncan?

Oh, how could he think I'd prefer Dunc the Skunk over him? Duncan, who wore white T-shirts and dark green trousers held up by a narrow brown belt?

I slid into my seat next to Sarah. I poked my spoon into the dish of grapefruit and orange sections.

I put down my spoon.

I gazed across the table at Lou, not seeing her, but looking past her. I touched my shoulder, briefly, dreamily. I will never wash this shoulder again. Not as long as I can feel the touch of his hand on it. Silly! I told myself. Dumb!

But I could feel his hand, almost as if it were still resting easily on my shoulder.

I raced back to the bunk after supper and ripped off my Gemini T-shirt. He'll notice you changed clothes, I told myself. Do you want him to think you changed clothes for him?

He can think whatever he wants, I answered myself, as long as he thinks I look beautiful. And anyway, we always go to get sweaters before evening activity. Just a T-shirt is too light for nighttime here.

I put on my yellow and blue plaid shirt with the white collar and a yellow wool sweater. My jeans looked better on me than any other pants I had so I left them on. I used Joanie's mirror to put on peach frost lipstick and a little blusher. I stared at myself in the mirror. *Why* hadn't I washed my hair? It looked positively *stringy*.

Someone tapped me on the shoulder and I whirled around.

"Lou!"

"Who'd you expect? Are you through with that mirror? The bathroom's a madhouse."

"Listen, can I borrow your dry shampoo? You have that spray stuff, don't you?"

"Sure, in my cubby. Go ahead."

I sprayed my hair with the white powder and brushed hard to get all of it out. It smelled nice and my hair looked a little better but it felt kind of stiff and wasn't nearly as shiny as it is after I wash it.

But it would have to do. At the last minute I remembered I wanted to put on cologne so I had to dab wherever I could reach, which wasn't too many places, since I was pretty well covered up. I pulled my shirt collar out and sprinkled a little on the front of my neck.

"That smells nice," sniffed Lou appreciatively. "Very fresh and youthful."

Youthful! Who wanted to smell youthful?

"You want some?"

"No thanks. I have my own." Lou waved a black bottle with gold lettering on it. "My Sin."

Lou wasn't going to smell youthful, that was for sure.

"Do we get to sit with the boys at the movie?" I asked her, my voice almost a whisper.

"Depends. If we're quiet about it and don't mess around they usually don't bother us. Why?"

"Well, somebody asked me to save him a seat and—"

"Dunc?"

"No. But can I do that? Can we save seats?"

"*Steve?*" She patted me on the shoulder. I wished she'd stop touching that shoulder. I felt like jumping out of my skin when she did. That was *Steve's* shoulder.

"Good work!" she said.

What work, I wondered?

"Can I?"

"The best thing to do," she advised, "is to meet

him outside the Rec Hall and walk in with him. All the Seniors sit in the last row so you just kind of casually sit down together. Everybody else will be doing it too."

"I don't want to look like I'm waiting for him."

"That's okay. He knows his way around. He'll probably be waiting for you."

He was. Right in front of the steps of the Rec Hall. He'd put on a blue warmup jacket over his shirt.

"Hi," he said.

"Hi." I couldn't think of anything more to say. Just being next to Steve seemed to dry up my throat and make words disappear.

We went inside and headed for the last row of benches. Sarah and Alan were sitting together already and we slid in beside them.

No one stopped us.

The lights went off. The movie started.

It was called *The Cockeyed Quarterback*. It was about a high school football star who changes into the team mascot—a goat. I don't remember too much of it because a minute after the lights went off Steve took my hand.

His hand was cool as he locked his fingers firmly with mine. As the movie progressed I could feel my hand getting warmer and warmer, till it felt positively sticky. I wished he would let it go so I could wipe it off. What would he think of someone whose palms were so sticky? Then he put his other hand over mine, holding my hand in both of his. He squeezed gently. I forgot all about my palms being sticky. Now I had to concentrate on keeping my inhaling and exhaling as quiet as possible. I didn't want him to hear how much trouble I was having just breathing normally.

Everyone around us was laughing at the quarterback turned goat. Especially when he galloped for the winning touchdown with the ball tucked under his chin, butting everyone in his path with his horns.

The lights went on.

"Like the movie?" asked Steve.

What movie?

"If I never saw another Walt Disney comedy—" Alan said in disgust.

"Don't complain," Steve said. "We saw this twice last year. It's getting to be what you call a Camp Timberwood Classic."

He let go of my hand. Plop, just like that, it dropped back at my side. I will never wash this hand again, I vowed, but I was grateful for the chance to rub it against my jeans when Steve wasn't looking. It was like a magic cord had been cut and now that we were no longer tied together with it, I could think calmly again.

And the first calm thought I had was: I have to speak to him about Dougie.

Everyone trooped to the mess hall where punch and cookies were set out on a long table. We got ours and took it out next to the back door; we stood there under the light with Sarah and Alan.

Now, I thought. You promised, and this is the only chance you'll get.

I didn't want to. It was none of my business. I didn't want to do anything to disturb the romantic feelings that an hour and a half of hand-holding had stirred up.

But I'd promised.

Ricky came out of the mess hall, followed by a husky boy with dark, curly hair. He seemed to be hanging on her, trailing after her like a puppy. She took one look at us, turned, and said, "Come on, Norman."

She headed toward the front of the mess hall and Norman obediently trotted after her. The only thing missing was a friendly "Arf."

I looked up at Steve, wondering where to begin about Dougie. He was grinning.

"Good old Norman," he said. "I knew he'd like Ricky."

I puzzled over this for a moment. Then, slowly, I began to understand. "At the dance last night," I said timidly.

"You were with Dunc so much—" He left the sentence unfinished.

"Well, Ricky was reading your palm—"

"Now Ricky can read Norman's palm."

"Did you—I mean, you know—set this up? Between Norman and Ricky?"

He just kept on grinning. He *had* liked me all along! Only, he thought I liked Duncan and I just stayed with Duncan because I thought he liked Ricky. But he had only stayed with Ricky because he couldn't find a way to get loose from her.

I sighed happily.

Anne and Harvey came around to the side of the mess hall.

"Time to go, kids," Anne said.

We dumped our paper cups in the trash basket and Steve put his arm around me.

Cool, calm, straight-thinking me disappeared, replaced by teeth-chattering, shivering me. Think calmly? Ha! My calmest thought was that now, besides not being able to wash one shoulder and one hand, I would have to give up washing the upper part of my right arm. It was going to be hard to take a shower and keep my whole right side dry.

With a struggle, I cleared all nuttiness from my mind. I took a deep breath.

"Your brother's in my swimming group," I began. I really didn't want to do this.

"Yeah, I know. I've seen you."

"Oh." We were halfway to the bunk. I *had* to plunge right in. I'd *promised*.

"He's kind of unhappy. I talked to him yesterday. He was sitting outside the Arts and Crafts shack all alone."

"The kid's a pain," he said impatiently.

"Steve! He was waiting for *you*. He was going to wait there forever, if he had to, until you came along."

He stopped short. He dropped his arm from around my shoulder and stuffed his hands in his pockets. "Melanie, why are we talking about my brother?"

"Because I promised him I would. He begged me to talk to you. Don't you realize how miserable he is?"

"Great," he said angrily. "That's just great. Now he's got another sucker to baby him."

Joanie came up behind us. "Move it along, kids, move it along."

He started walking again, but he kept his hands in his pockets.

I felt lost without his arm around me. I had made him angry, I had loused everything up, just as it was getting started. But how could he be so mean? How could he call me a sucker for wanting to help a little kid?

"Steve, he's your *brother*. Maybe it's none of my business, but—"

"That's right!" he snapped. "It's none of your business."

I was too shocked at the anger in his voice and the nastiness of his reply to talk. I was close to tears. How could he change so much in a matter of minutes? Just because I mentioned his brother?

58

"I'm sorry," he said finally. His voice was low. "But he's a baby, Mel, and he's got to learn not to come running to me, or you or anyone else to help him get out of things. He's got to learn to stand on his own two feet. He's been babied too long as it is."

"Steve, he's only — what? — seven years old?"

"Almost eight. And when he's ten? Eleven? If he doesn't start now, he'll never learn to stand up for himself. I won't always be around to make it easy for him."

"I don't see you making it easy for him now," I retorted.

"You don't understand," he said, sounding defeated. "You really don't."

"No, I don't."

"He did want me to get him out of something, didn't he?"

"Well — yes. Arts and Crafts. But all the kids were making fun of him—"

"Yeah. That's what I figured."

We were back at the bunk now.

"You were waiting to talk to me about him, weren't you, Mel?"

"What do you mean? I promised him I would, yes."

"Well, if I tell you I don't want to talk about Doug, what happens then?"

I didn't understand what he meant. I couldn't see what he was getting at.

We stood at the side of the bunk, the light from the windows shining out in a pool around us. I studied his face, but I couldn't see much there except a frown.

"If you hadn't promised Doug you'd talk to me, would you be here with me right now?"

"Oh, yes!" I blurted out, without thinking. I forgot completely about being cool.

"That's all I wanted to know," he said. "I just like to know where I stand."

He brushed my cheek with his fingers, lightly, almost as if he wanted to make sure that I was actually *there*. Then he turned and walked off, leaving me standing alone under the window.

I stared after him, absolutely bewildered over the whole evening. I touched my cheek and sighed. I felt dreamy and silly and muddled.

I went into the bunk slowly and headed straight for my cot. I will never, I thought, wash this cheek again, either.

Then I laughed out loud.

SIX

S arah and I were officially
Frogs now and we were learning the overhand crawl.
As soon as we could do two laps of the crawl without
stopping we would be Sunfish and allowed out of the
Frog Pond.

Doug and Jason were still Tadpoles because they
couldn't float for ten seconds, but as Sarah and I prac-
ticed through the next week, I wondered why in the
world I wanted to get to the other side of that rope
anyway.

Ricky had doubled, maybe tripled, her attacks on
me. Now that Steve was definitely mine, she had even
more reason to hate me. She was jealous. She was
especially good at sneak attacks, striking when I least
expected it.

The most unlikely thing could set her off.

Like, one afternoon she was sitting on her cot,
shaving her legs with a disposable razor and no soap
or lather at all. You could hear the scrape of the razor
all across the bunk. I came in from the bathroom, a
towel wrapped around me, still dripping from the

shower. (I decided that it would be impractical to leave all those parts of me unwashed.) I heard this scraping sound. I looked over at Ricky and I guess I stared.

"What's the matter, Melanie, don't you know about shaving your legs yet?"

"Without soap?"

"Without soap?" Ricky mimicked, in a high-pitched whine. "It doesn't hurt, Melanie. You ought to try it some time." She looked down at my bare, wet legs and wrinkled her nose. "You really *ought* to try it some time. Does your mommy let you shave yet?"

She made me feel so stupid. I never saw anybody shave *anything* without some kind of lather, unless they were using an electric razor. I'd only shaved my legs a couple of times, like when I was going to wear skirts without dark panty hose or something. Most of the time my legs didn't show, so my mother urged me to put off regular shaving as long as possible. Not because she didn't want me to, but because she said it was a pain in the neck and I might as well delay it as long as I could.

But now that I was wearing shorts so much — maybe Ricky was right . . .

I went back into the bathroom to finish drying off, making sure first to take some clothes from my cubby with me. I didn't want Ricky sitting there looking at the rest of my body, saying God knows what about each separate part.

"Hey, Mel," she called after me, "don't be shy. You've got nothing to hide. And I mean *nothing*."

I cringed. One of the things about her was that she always seemed to know where your weak spots were — at least, my weak spots. It was almost like she could read my mind.

Joanie was in the bathroom, about to step into the shower.

"She's a real pain, isn't she?" she said sympathetically.

"Yeah." I dried myself off, trying not to show how upset I was.

"Just ignore her."

"I've been ignoring her!" I blurted out. "It doesn't do any good. She never stops."

"Somebody ought to have a long talk with that girl," Joan muttered. She stepped into the shower. "I'll see what Anne thinks."

I wish someone *would* have a long talk with Ricky, I thought bitterly. A long talk followed by a short right to the jaw.

And then there was Dougie.

I told him I had talked to his brother, like I promised. But once I told him that, I didn't know what else to say. I didn't want to tell him what Steve had said, and there was nothing I could do to make him understand that his brother wanted me to keep out of it.

So I just told him that Steve thought it would be best for him to *try*.

"Try what?" Dougie asked. "Try lanyards?"

"Try whatever it is the rest of the kids are doing. Just do the best you can."

I felt helpless. I was sorry for Dougie, and really wanted to do something to make it better for him, but I didn't know what to do.

I also felt a little guilty, because I had a feeling that if I didn't like his brother so much, I might be more willing to stand up for Dougie and make a big enough stink so that Steve might give in.

But it really isn't any of my business, I kept telling myself. Steve knows his brother better than I do. It's not that he doesn't care about Dougie. He's probably just doing what he thinks is best for him.

I don't know if I really believed that, though I wanted to believe it. I didn't want to think that Steve was rotten. I didn't want to be in love with a heartless rat.

Because I *was* in love. I was sure of it. Steve was such an absolutely perfect person, as anybody in her right mind could see, that it was impossible not to be in love with him. He never fumbled or stumbled; he always seemed so sure of himself, so in control of everything. Even when he said he wanted to know where he stood, even when he asked me if I'd be with him if I hadn't promised Dougie to talk to him, he didn't act nervous or uncertain about what I'd tell him. It was just, he wanted to know, and whatever I said, that would be that.

If it had been me, I don't think I even would have had the nerve to ask the question. I would have been too scared to hear what the answer was. I don't think Steve was scared of anything.

And he was so intelligent. I mean, he *never* said dumb things; he was a thinker. Maybe he didn't talk a whole lot, but when he did he always sounded right. He had a sense of humor too and it wasn't a silly one. He was witty, but he didn't always feel like he had to make a joke. And he was never, *ever* dopey.

I never knew a boy like Steve before. Sometimes I wondered, on and off, why a perfect person would be in love with me. I was so different from him. Steve would never refuse to put his face in the lake and blow bubbles. Steve would never have trouble getting his foot up high enough to reach a stirrup. Steve didn't seem to have any trouble with his breathing at all when he was holding my hand.

Sometimes I also wondered, on and off, whether he actually *was* in love with me. (Steve never would have wondered about that, either.) Whenever I began thinking that way, I reminded myself of one of my father's favorite sayings: "Don't look a gift horse in the mouth."

(Steve has beautiful teeth, too.)

Anyway, since he was so perfect I told myself that he *couldn't* be a heartless rat and it was very sensible of me to be in love with him and that he really was concerned that Dougie learn to *adjust*.

I talked the whole thing over with Sarah and she agreed.

As for Dougie, he didn't hold a grudge. After one swim period he seemed to get over his disappointment in me. He didn't mention lanyards again and he stuck as close to me as ever.

It seemed like ages since the night at the movies and I'd hardly seen Steve at all; we didn't have any daytime activities together and the evening activities had been things like the Camp Timberwood Sing, where each bunk performs a couple of songs and the best bunk wins; and camp fires with marshmallow toasting and more singing and Uncle Howie and some of the other counselors telling ghost stories. They made us stay with our own bunks most of the time. The best we could do was meet outside the mess hall before meals, and then only for a couple of minutes.

The day before visiting day I got two letters from home, one from my father and one from my mother. They were postmarked over a week before.

Dear Melanie,

We tried to call you twice after we got your last letter, but once they said you were already asleep and once you were down at the waterfront and now the camp phone is out and we can't get through at all. We were worried about your homesickness. I really

65

didn't think you would miss us as much as we missed you, what with all the things to keep you busy there. How could you imagine that we don't miss you like mad? I didn't want to bother you with it, or make you feel responsible, if you know what I mean, but I guess it was a mistake not to let you know my real feelings, because by not telling you I see I've upset you more than if I'd told you.

The truth is, Daddy and I both feel lonely for you every single day. We don't go around moping and crying, exactly, but the apartment is much more quiet than we're used to and it's a very strange feeling not having you come home at three, or at least, not being all together at dinner.

I hope by this time you're feeling better—I'm sure you must be—but if you're not, please call us if you want to talk. Tell Uncle Dan I said so—you're to call any time you want, collect.

In any case, we'll see you on the 26th and we can't wait. We'll start out very early, so we ought to be up at camp by ten A.M., which is when they want us to arrive.

See you soon!

Love, love, love,
Mom

The one from my father said practically the same thing, but he added some stuff about trying to be independent and keeping my chin up.

Boy, did I feel guilty.

I'd sent them two postcards since the letter I'd written about the dance but the mail was so slow they hadn't gotten them. To tell the truth, I'd hardly thought of my parents at all for quite a while. I was looking forward to their visit tomorrow, of course, but I'd only begun to get excited about that *today*. My homesickness was completely cured; instead of mooning over my parents I was mooning over Steve, and between all the activities and looking for him every time I went from one place to the other, I had barely a spare moment to think about home.

And I didn't have time now, either, because rest hour was just about over and I had to get ready for my riding lesson. Karen had said I might go on the trail today. Either that or start cantering. I decided if I had a choice I'd go on the trail, because cantering is almost as fast as galloping and it might be a little dangerous. I thought it would be a shame if my parents had to spend Visiting Day visiting me in the infirmary watching my bones set.

Down at the ring Karen greeted me cheerfully. "Marlon can't wait to canter," she announced. (Marlon was what she finally named my nice old horse when I kept insisting that I wanted to call him something besides "Horse.")

"Gee, he doesn't look eager to me." Marlon was sleeping standing up, lazily flicking his tail at a fly, but not very often.

"How are you, Marlon?" I asked, patting his shoulder. He yawned.

"A couple of trots around the ring and he'll be wide awake," Karen promised.

I mounted Marlon. It was easier to get my foot up now, but still a big stretch. I trotted him around the ring, posting as Karen had taught me. You have to raise and lower yourself in the stirrups, in rhythm with the horse's shoulder movements. It takes a while to get coordinated, and at first I got some pretty good jolts, going down when I should have gone up. But that was when I was just starting to learn. By now I'd been trotting so long I posted perfectly. So perfectly, in fact, that Karen — and maybe Marlon — was getting bored with my trotting and eager to move me on to cantering.

"Good! Good!" Karen cried. "Beautiful. Couldn't be better. You're really getting to look terrific on that horse, Mel."

I was proud — but suspicious. I had a feeling she was pouring on the praise to set me up for going out into the field and starting to canter.

"You're definitely ready to move on," Karen declared.

"Karen, could I please ride the trail? I'm really dying to go on the trail. It would be a nice change from just going around the ring."

She gave me a knowing little smile. "So would cantering," she said. "But if you want to, we'll go on the trail today and leave the cantering till next week. But next week *for sure,* and no excuses."

I was so relieved that I didn't have to canter today that I could almost make myself believe that once Visiting Day was over I'd actually look forward to learning how.

Karen mounted the second horse, who was sometimes in the ring with Marlon. "I'll lead. Marlon is a pretty good follower."

"Yours won't break into a run or anything, will he?" I asked nervously.

"No. We'll just walk. The trail's a little steep. And besides, we don't want to annoy the bees."

She led the way out of the ring.

"Bees?" I called after her. *"Bees?"*

"I think they're pretty much cleared out," she called back. "But you never know with bees. Anyway, if you see any, don't panic. Just stay still."

I stayed still. I was frozen to the saddle. It was a good thing we were walking instead of trotting so that

68

I didn't have to post. Otherwise, my up and down, up and down might have upset the bees.

Marlon *was* a good follower. The trail wasn't that steep but it was downhill and it was up to Marlon to keep his footing, to keep from slipping and to keep an eye on Karen's horse, because I was too busy checking the low-hanging branches of the trees on either side of the trail for beehives. The only thing I moved were my eyeballs, side to side, up and down. I might have missed a very pleasant ride for all I know, because the next thing I knew, we were coming out of the wooded area of the trail and approaching the lake.

I breathed a sigh of relief, and relaxed. Karen's horse strolled down to the edge of the water and got his hooves wet. He bent his neck forward and took a few delicate sips of the lake.

Marlon pricked up his ears and raised his head. Suddenly he seemed very interested in his surroundings. He almost trotted to the edge of the water, although I hadn't kicked him. He stood for a moment, drinking, as the water lapped gently against his hooves.

"Nothing like a nice drink of lake on a hot day, eh, Marlon?" I murmured. I patted his mane.

Then, instead of turning around and coming out of the water, Marlon began to move forward. He waded into the lake until the water was up to his ankles— or whatever it is horses have where people have their ankles.

"That's enough, Marlon," I scolded. "Come on out."

"Don't talk to him, Melanie," said Karen. "He's not a dog. Use the reins and your knees."

"I *am* using the reins. He's not listening!"

Marlon moved deeper into the lake.

I tugged the reins back again, a little harder. "Enough's enough, Marlon," I pleaded. I pulled the left rein and nudged him with my left foot to get him to turn around toward shore. Marlon shook his head impatiently. He splashed on, into the lake.

I began to feel the beginnings of panic. This dumb horse was out of control. Not only was I going to flunk horseback riding because I couldn't make Marlon do a simple thing like turn around and walk out of a lake, but it was possible that I would drown if Marlon decided to walk right across the whole lake to the swimming area on the other side.

Maybe I ought to get off right *now,* I thought.

The water was up to Marlon's knees — or whatever.

"Karen!" Should I jump off and try to lead him back? My beautiful riding boots would be ruined. But, on the other hand, my mother would probably rather have me ruin my boots than die.

"Don't panic, Mel. And stop shouting. He's just cooling himself off. He'll come out when he's ready."

"He's supposed to come out when *I'm* ready!"

It was too late to tell me not to panic, because I had passed through panic and was now verging on hysteria. While I couldn't make up my mind about whether or not to jump off Marlon, he was single-mindedly plunging onward. Marlon was going to cool himself very thoroughly, and me with him. I didn't need any cooling off. The day was hot but I was shivering.

Now the water was up to the stirrups. The heels of my boots were submerged. Since they were going to get wet anyway I decided to get off while the getting was good. The water was up to my waist here, but if I waited any longer . . .

Only, Marlon kept moving; farther and farther into the lake. And I didn't know how to get down off a moving horse. I was sure the stirrups would jiggle and I would fall.

"Stop, Marlon!" I tugged on the reins. I was clutching them so tightly that my fingernails dug into my palms, leaving little dents. *"Stop!"*

Marlon didn't stop. The stirrup floated out from under my left foot. It was too late to get off. Now I was certain. Marlon *did* mean to go clear across the lake until he reached the other side. Imagine the surprise of the kids at General Swim when they realize there's a horse calmly paddling toward them. A horse with an empty saddle.

"GIRL AND HORSE INVOLVED IN BIZARRE ACCIDENT!" the headlines would shriek. "HORSE OKAY."

"Karen, do something! I can't swim!"

"Don't worry. The horse can."

Marlon stopped to drink. The water lapped around the saddle and sloshed over my thighs. He hardly had to bend his head at all.

Through a haze of terror I could hear Karen laughing on shore.

"It isn't funny!" I shrieked. "Karen, I'm *scared!*"

"Melanie, please calm down. He'll come out in a minute."

And sure enough, when Marlon finished drinking he raised his head and looked around, almost as if he were trying to figure out where he was and how he'd gotten here.

And then, slowly, lazily, he turned around and began to head for dry land.

Weak with relief, I slumped in the saddle as we moved into shallow water. My fear gradually began to dissolve, but I was shaking when we reached the shore.

I was furious at Karen.

She was still laughing.

"It wasn't funny," I said.

"Come on, Mel, it was. And there's no harm done."

"I'm soaked. My boots are ruined. I could have *drowned*. Isn't that enough harm? You should have done something."

"Put newspaper in your boots. And you wouldn't have drowned."

We started back up the trail to the ring. I didn't speak to Karen all the way back and I wasn't speaking to Marlon either. He was his old self again, calmly following Karen's horse. My wet jeans clung to my legs, my boots were waterlogged. I didn't even think about bees. I just sagged in the saddle with the reins hanging limply in my hands. I didn't even try to steer Marlon.

We returned to the ring and Marlon stopped in front of his spot on the rail. I dismounted. My legs nearly gave way as my boots touched the ground. I was still shaken, but now that I wasn't in immediate danger of death, I felt more rage at Karen than anything else. The water sloshed in my boots and I pulled them off, one at a time, hopping to keep my balance. I dumped the water on the ground and struggled to pull the boots back on. It wasn't easy and they felt awfully uncomfortable. But I couldn't walk all the way back without shoes. Once I got through the wooded area and onto the main campus, where it was mostly grassy, I'd take them off.

"You'd better go back to your bunk and change," Karen advised.

I gave her my nastiest look.

"See you tomorrow," she said cheerfully. We were going to give a riding demonstration for the parents.

"Yeah. See you," I muttered.

Without a backward glance at the ring I walked off.

My boots felt awful. By the time I reached the main campus my feet were aching and I sank down on the grass to pull the boots off. With a sigh of relief I wiggled my toes, then hauled myself up. With a boot in each hand I limped toward Bunk 7.

The campus was deserted. The activity period hadn't ended yet and except for a group of little kids all the way down near the tetherball pole next to Bunk 1, there wasn't a camper or counselor in sight.

I figured I had about fifteen minutes to relax and get myself cleaned up and back to normal before the rest of my bunk returned from Arts and Crafts.

"Mel?"

I whirled around.

"Steve!"

"What happened to *you?*"

Oh, what timing! I could have cried. For days I'd been longing to run into him, to have just a couple of moments with him between activities and now here he was—at probably the only time in my life I didn't want to see him. Or really, didn't want *him* to see *me*.

Because even though I looked like a half-drowned rat and felt ridiculous and was wearing my crummiest jeans which didn't look good even when they weren't sticking soggily to my thighs, my heart couldn't help doing that swoop down into my stomach at the sight of him.

"How'd you get wet?"

"It's a long story." So he *did* notice how awful I looked. Of course he noticed. How could he *not* notice? *Nobody* could not notice that I was soaked from the bottom of my T-shirt to the frayed ends of my jeans, and that I dripped as I walked.

"What are you doing here?" I asked stupidly.

73

"I was helping out in the canteen, getting it ready for tomorrow. Did you fall out of a canoe?"

He walked next to me as I headed for my bunk.

"No. Believe it or not, I was at my riding lesson."

"You got wet riding?"

Maybe it *was* funny. Maybe Steve would think it was funny.

"Well, see, my horse decided he wanted to cool off a little. It gets hot in that ring, you know? And it *is* a very hot day."

"Yeah? So?"

"Well, we went down the trail to the lake and Marlon—"

"Marlon?"

"My horse. Marlon took one look at all that water and realized that he was dying for a dip in the lake. So we dipped."

"He went *swimming?* With you on him?"

We'd reached the bunk. I sank down on a porch step. Steve sat down next to me.

"He didn't exactly swim," I said. "It was more like wading—up to the neck."

Steve began to smile. "It's a funny picture," he said, almost apologetically.

"You should have been there. Karen nearly died laughing."

A bugle call suddenly blared out over the PA, signaling the end of the activity period.

"Well," said Steve, "everybody'll be back in a minute. I guess you want to change."

"Yeah. I really do." Though I hadn't thought much about my general sogginess for the past couple of minutes.

"Well. I'll see you."

I didn't want him to leave.

"Your parents coming tomorrow?" I asked. I dangled a boot casually from two fingers.

"Yeah. Yours?"

"Uh huh."

"Maybe you can meet them," he said, looking down at the boot. "I'd like to — you know, if we get a chance — I'm sure they want to meet you."

I dropped the boot. My fingers fluttered, almost trembling, as if they were waving 'bye-'bye to my boot.

He wanted me to meet his parents! Wasn't that practically like saying he was thinking of *marrying* me?

Oh, don't be dumb! I told myself. I'm thirteen, for heaven's sake. He's fifteen. I'm not even as old as Juliet was when she married Romeo, and everyone knows that she was fourteen and therefore practically a *baby*.

The campus was now alive with activity. A whole cluster of my bunkmates was approaching.

I couldn't think of another thing to say.

"Well, see you," said Steve.

"Okay." He touched my shoulder lightly and walked off toward Bunk 8.

Sarah and Reenie said hi to him as they passed, then strolled toward me with knowing smiles on their faces. I reached for my boots and stood up. The girls stopped short and stared at my wetness.

"What happened to *you?*" Sarah demanded.

I sighed, and grinned a silly grin. "It's a long story."

SEVEN

Visiting day was almost a blur as we raced from one activity to another, showing off our accomplishments. I wondered every once in a while if our parents could tell us apart and if they knew who they were clapping for, because Uncle Dan had told us we all had to wear our camp Timberwood T-shirts.

"Let's really show them that old Camp Timberwood spirit," he urged us that morning at flag raising. "And in case any of you need a Camp Timberwood shirt, come up to the main house right after breakfast. They're only six dollars, and your parents can pay me when they get here."

The bunk bulged with parents and "Care Packages" of cake and candy. Everybody's package had to be opened and laid out on the bed to be inspected by everybody else.

My parents arrived a few minutes before ten, just as we finished a very thorough clean-up. I flung myself at them wildly, not realizing until that moment that I really *had* missed them, even when I thought I hadn't.

"We got your cards," my mother said, after they

finished hugging and kissing me. "We were so relieved."

"I knew you'd be okay," my father said proudly. "When do we get to see you swim?"

"Let's meet your friends," my mother suggested. "And where is Anne?"

It was a madhouse all day. In fact, I decided that Visiting Day meant that my parents saw more of me than I saw of them. Because I spent the day performing—my face float, my back float, my trotting, etc., while they watched me.

My father was overjoyed with my face float. He couldn't get over it. "For years she wouldn't put her face in the water," he kept telling my mother. "For *years*. Now look at her. She's practically swimming." (I'd also showed him what little I could do of the overhand crawl, which I was just beginning to learn.)

My mother was thrilled when we had the riding demonstration. Although I was still not speaking to Karen, Karen introduced me as "one of our most promising beginners, who is going to be a fine rider very soon." I think she was trying to butter me up. Maybe she was worried that I'd tell my parents how she almost let me drown yesterday. All I did was walk around the ring on Marlon and then trot him, once around, turn and trot the other way. My mother thought that was wonderful. I was glad Marlon obeyed me today. He seemed back to normal, so I forgave him and patted him as I dismounted.

"I don't even know how you climb up on that thing!" my mother marveled. "He's so big. Isn't he an awfully big horse?"

"Nah," I said casually, "he's just your basic horse."

We had lunch in shifts and we got to sit with our families at any table we wanted. Sarah and I introduced our parents to each other and we ate together, along with Anne and Ricky and her parents. I don't know how it worked out that way, but there we were. They just sat down with us.

Ricky's father, Mr. Stone, was a talker. Practically a speechmaker. He talked about his business. Once he asked Sarah's father about his job, but then he launched into a long description of his own shoe factory. (Stone Shoes! How uncomfortable, I thought, and nearly giggled.) Ricky was very quiet all through lunch. In fact, she didn't say a word. Neither did her mother; actually, nobody got to say very much except for Mr. Stone.

Coming out of the mess hall after lunch we bumped into Steve and Dougie and their parents coming in.

"Hey, Mel!" cried Dougie. Before Steve could say anything, Dougie was introducing me to his parents. "Mel's in my swimming group," he said. "She's my friend."

I glanced over at my father who was frowning. I think he was kind of let down to realize that this little kid and I were in the same swimming group. Mr. and Mrs. Tepper, on the other hand, looked delighted. It all depends on your point of view, I guess.

Steve didn't say a word. He just stood there with a strange smile on his face and let Dougie do all the talking. This wasn't exactly the way I'd pictured meeting Steve's parents.

"It's nice to meet you, Melanie," said Mrs. Tepper. "Dougie certainly seems to have made a good friend."

"Yes, well, Dougie's a very nice boy," I said stupidly.

Steve wasn't smiling now, but Dougie positively beamed.

We all stood there for a moment, till I realized I should introduce my parents to Steve and *his* parents.

But what should I say? Steve wasn't going to say anything. I mean, he didn't point out that I was his friend too, and he didn't seem to be on the verge of telling his father that I was the girl he planned to marry. At least, not right this minute.

"Um, this is Steve Tepper," I said finally. "This is my mother and father, Mr. and Mrs. Kessler."

I practically mumbled the whole introduction. It was awful, not at all the way it should have been. I would have introduced them to Aunt Rosalind with as much enthusiasm. But what else could I say? If Steve didn't tell his parents that I was his girl friend, I couldn't tell my parents he was my boy friend.

"See you later, Mel." There was something about the way Steve said it that made the words sound a lot better than your ordinary "See you later." Steve said it so that it came out like "I *will* see you later, for sure."

I must have lit up like a spotlight, because as soon as the Teppers had gone into the mess hall my mother remarked, too casually, "What a nice-looking boy." Then she watched my face for a reaction.

"Yeah. He's a friend of mine." I tried to sound just as casual as she did.

Why didn't I tell them Steve was my boy friend? I wondered about that on and off the rest of the afternoon. I'd always told them practically everything that was on my mind, sharing my problems with them, and they'd always encouraged me to. But this time . . . I don't know. I just didn't feel like discussing Steve with them. For some reason I preferred talking about him to Sarah than to my mother and father. It was strange, this sudden secret-keeping. I wasn't used to it.

The afternoon sped by too fast. We visited the Arts and Crafts shack, where my parents admired a spatter painting I'd made and took home a lumpy, Day-Glo yellow ashtray in the shape of a human kidney. My mother swore she'd display it on the coffee table.

"You don't have to go *that* far, Mom," I said. "Besides, you guys don't even smoke."

"Nonetheless," she insisted. I shrugged. It really was a terrible ashtray.

We had a parent-daughter softball game, but lost most of the fathers by the third inning. (Most of the mothers weren't too thrilled about it to begin with.) Mr. Stone had a wonderful time. "Talk it up!" he kept urging. "Let's hear a little enthusiasm out here!" Ricky talked it up, but she was practically meek in comparison to her usual self.

Ricky hit four home runs, which pleased her father no end. By a fluke, I managed a double; I also struck out three times, but somehow my parents overlooked the strikeouts and just seemed to notice the double.

At five o'clock it was time for them to go.

They hugged and kissed me and told me what a good time they'd had, and how proud of me they were. My mother patted her big canvas tote bag to remind me that she still had my ashtray in there.

"See you in a couple of weeks," my father said.

I almost started to cry. I didn't want them to go. I walked them out onto the porch, where Anne and Joanie were saying good-bye to the others. Everybody was leaving now, and I wasn't the only one who looked close to tears.

Diane was standing next to Ricky, whose parents had just left, actually clinging to her mother's arm as if to keep her from going. Mrs. Turner kept patting her on the shoulder while she talked to Anne.

I took a deep breath and kissed my parents again. "Good-bye. Write."

I watched them walk away. Mrs. Turner followed.

"Come inside," said Anne. "Come on, everyone inside. There's about two tons of food in there and if you kids don't decide what to do with it I'm going to confiscate the whole lot."

The magic words. Instead of tearfully watching our parents grow smaller as they walked farther and farther away from us, we scrambled back into the bunk to protect our loot.

"Did anybody get a salami?" asked Lou. "I would *kill* for a salami."

"Why didn't you tell your mother to bring one?" asked Audrey.

"I didn't think of it."

"Your parents are nice," said Sarah, collecting all the stuff she'd piled on her bed.

"Thanks. So are yours." To tell the truth, I didn't really get that clear an impression of Sarah's parents. They were awfully quiet, like Sarah, and seemed pretty serious. All I knew was that Mr. Felton was a watch and clock repairer and Mrs. Felton was a piano teacher.

My parents had brought pistachio nuts, white chocolate, sourballs, bakery cookies, potato chips and cheese crackers.

"I'll trade anybody *anything* for a salami," Lou wailed, sounding desperate.

"What have you got?" asked Reenie.

Lou jumped up. "Have you got a salami?"

"No. You want some M and M's?"

Lou sank back onto her cot dejectedly. "You're the kind of person," she grumbled, "who'd give a person dying of thirst a nice glass of sand."

"I'm terribly sorry," said Reenie, her voice haughty.

Anne was serious about confiscating our food. We put it all back in the packages and bags it had come in. She said anything that was opened had to be finished up tonight. As long as we kept the other stuff

81

in sealed packages, we could store it temporarily in our cubbies.

"We don't," she said firmly, "want rats."

"Oh, Anne," Audrey scoffed, "we do this every year and we never get rats."

"If Uncle Dan knew I was letting you keep any of this stuff in here—"

"All right, all right." Audrey gave in.

We had a cookout that night for dinner. I guess it was supposed to cheer us up. We sat on blankets and had hamburgers and hot dogs and cole slaw and corn on the cob and fruit punch.

We were just settling down with our paper plates when Reenie cried, "Yeck! There's an ant in my cole slaw!" She jumped up and took her plate to Uncle Dan, who was standing over the long table of salads and things.

"Uncle Dan, there's an ant in my cole slaw," she complained.

"This is a *cookout*," he said.

"Yeah, but there's an *ant* in my food. Can I have another plate of cole slaw?"

"You didn't finish this one," he pointed out.

"But there's an ant in it!" She was practically yelling.

Uncle Dan reached over, took his index finger and went *flick* right over her cole slaw. He smiled sweetly. "Now there isn't," he said.

Reenie stormed back to the blanket. "I'm not eating this," she said. "Do you believe that?"

"Sure we believe it," said Carol. "At least he didn't pull his old, 'Oh, Reenie, how much can an ant eat?' routine."

"I know he's a cheapskate," said Reenie, "but one lousy lump of cole slaw?"

The Senior Boys, carrying plates and dragging blankets, were heading our way.

"There's Alan," I said to Sarah.

"Move over," she whispered. "Make room."

I moved over, nearly knocking Diane into her fruit punch. "Move over," I said. "Leave a little room, okay?"

She glared at me. She didn't move.

"Hi, Mel." Steve was looking down at me. "Hold my plate a minute, will you?" I held his plate.

He spread his blanket. Diane didn't even have to move, because he just created a new space opposite me. He sat down and I handed him back his plate.

Alan settled between Sarah and me.

"Hello, Melanie," he said politely. He was as serious as Sarah was.

"Hello, Alan. Did you have a nice Visiting Day?"

"Well, Sarah got to meet my parents and I got to meet hers, so I guess it wasn't a total loss."

Sarah gazed at him with such admiration that you'd have thought he just said something brilliant.

I turned to Steve. "Your parents are nice. Your mother's very pretty."

"They thought *you* were wonderful," Steve said softly.

"They did? They hardly saw me for two minutes."

"Yeah, but Doug told them all about you. In *detail*."

"In detail? How much detail does he know?"

"Oh, plenty. About how you tried to save him from death by Arts and Crafts. Stuff like that."

"Ohh." Was he angry? Had his parents given him a hard time because of my interference? I wanted to know — but I didn't want to talk about Dougie. I just wanted Steve to tell me that it was all right, that he wasn't mad at me, that he would suffer any lecture from his mother, any disapproval from his father, that even if they *disinherited* him, he wouldn't care, as long as he knew I—

"Mel? Hey, Mel, someone's looking for you." Ricky led Dougie over to us. She smiled pleasantly. "Here you go," she said, plopping him down on my blanket, right between Steve and me.

Steve swore under his breath. I could have screamed, I was so frustrated.

But one look at Dougie and I melted. His eyes were bigger than ever and he kind of slumped over his plate. He didn't touch his food; he just sat there looking miserable.

Steve jabbed a fork into his cole slaw and started shoveling food into his mouth.

"What's the matter, Dougie?" I asked. "You feel a little down?"

"I'm homesick," he said.

"Well, sure you are. So am I."

I took a bite of my hamburger. "Hey, this is good," I said. "I'll bet that hot dog is good, too."

Dougie looked down at his hot dog. "You want it?" he offered.

"No, no, I just meant—Dougie, you better eat something."

"I'm not hungry."

"Doug, why don't you go back with your bunk?" Steve said. "That's where you belong."

"You're over here," Dougie said, "and this isn't your bunk."

"That's different," snapped Steve. "And most of my bunk *is* here."

I looked over Dougie's head at him. His eyes were cold and hard. I didn't like him looking that way.

"If you stay here will you eat something, Dougie?" I asked.

84

Steve shot me a look of pure fury. "He won't starve himself, Melanie, if that's what you're worried about. He never has yet."

I didn't like the way Steve was talking either. Maybe I'd been right way back at the beginning. Maybe he *was* a lousy brother. Why wasn't he trying to cheer Dougie up, instead of being so angry with him and so eager to get rid of him? Sure, I wanted to be alone with Steve, and sure, it gave me a major attack of goose pimples to know he wanted to be alone with me, but there was a very sad little kid here, crying out for help.

Dougie started to eat his corn.

"There you go. Isn't that good?" I glanced at Steve. He looked disgusted. I pleaded with him with my eyes to understand, tried to send him an ESP message to be patient. He looked away.

"Mind if we sit down?" cooed Ricky. Without waiting for an answer she squatted next to Steve and motioned Norman to sit down too.

("Down, Norman!" Norman sits. "Good dog.")

The only room for Norman was on the other side of Steve.

"Is this your brother?" Ricky asked. Steve nodded.

"What a cute little boy!" If I wasn't so angry, I would have laughed. Praising Dougie was not exactly the fastest route to Steve's heart.

Dougie wasn't too crazy about it either. He scowled at her.

Smart kid.

She chattered away at Steve. I talked to Dougie. Norman ate. Between bites, he tried to look around Steve to catch a glimpse of Ricky.

Steve began answering her. He got more and more lively as she talked. Ignoring Dougie and me, he gave all his attention to Ricky.

Dougie started to cheer up. He launched into a long description of all the things his parents had watched him do today. I listened with one ear and tried to keep the other ear on Steve and Ricky. Norman looked glum. I'm sure *I* looked glum. But three out of five of our cozy little circle were feeling terrific.

"Okay, Dougie," I said, "you'd better go back to your group now." Before things get out of hand, I thought grimly. Maybe they were already out of hand.

He'd finished all the food on his plate. He looked so much more cheerful that I managed to forget that a few minutes before I'd thought his brother was cold and heartless. "Joel will be looking for you."

"He knows I'm here. I told him. He said it was okay."

What a stupid counselor, I thought. He was doing nothing to help Dougie fit in with his own group. Instead of making the other kids stop picking on Dougie, he was letting him cling to his older brother and me. How was Dougie going to learn to get along with kids his own age if he was never with them?

But did I really want Dougie to go back to his bunkmates for his own good, or because I wanted to be alone with Steve before Ricky moved in and took over completely?

It didn't matter though, because here was Joel, coming to get him.

"Let's go, Doug. Time to go back to the bunk."

Dougie didn't argue or protest. He just said, " 'Bye, Mel," and went quietly.

Now, I thought, we can get down to business. I turned to Steve, and saw that he was just getting up with his empty plate. I got up too — with my half-full plate. Ricky got up. When Ricky got up, Norman got up. We looked like a bunch of jumping jacks.

"They're toasting marshmallows," Ricky said. "Want one, Mel?"

"I can get my own marshmallow," I said.

"Okay." She shrugged. "Then would you get me one, Steve?" she asked, trying to sound helpless. How ridiculous. She probably kept herself in shape by weight-lifting Volkswagens, but she couldn't carry a marshmallow ten feet.

"I'll get you one," Norman said. Ricky sat back down, a queen on her throne, to wait for her servants to bring her marshmallows.

Uncle Dan was doing the toasting at the barbecue pit; there was quite a line. We dumped our plates into a trash basket and went to wait our turns.

I took a deep breath and tried to pretend that Norman wasn't standing right next to us.

"Steve, don't be mad," I whispered.

"I'm not mad," he said pleasantly. He spoke in a normal tone of voice, loud enough for Norman to hear. "Why should I be mad?"

"Well, good. I just thought you might be—"

"If you're more worried about how my brother feels than about how I feel, I can't fight that."

I cringed. He didn't seem to care who heard him.

"I don't worry more about Dougie than you. That's not true."

"I don't know. That's the way it always seems to turn out."

"I told him to go," I said.

"Joel came to get him. He *had* to go."

"But I told him to first. Didn't you hear me?"

"No," he said blandly. "I was talking to Ricky."

We reached the front of the line. Uncle Dan held out one stick with one marshmallow on it.

"I need two," said Steve. "One is for a friend."

Uncle Dan eyed him suspiciously. "You're sure they're not both for you? It's only one at a time, you know."

Steve raised his right hand. "I swear. I don't even like marshmallows that much."

"You can come back for more," Uncle Dan said generously, "after you finish that. But only one at a time. And save your stick."

He went through the same routine with Norman. I only asked for one, although I saw by now that I could just as easily have gotten two. But I was rapidly falling out of the mood for marshmallows.

Steve and Norman each held out a stick with a marshmallow on it to Ricky. She rewarded Steve with a dazzling smile. To Norman she muttered, "Thanks."

I ate my marshmallow. It would have tasted a lot better if Steve had gotten it for me.

Anne and Joan were moving from blanket to blanket announcing the end of the cookout. Other counselors were gathering up the troops and heading back to their bunks. Sarah and Alan, Lou and Duncan and Carol and Jay Overgaard were already heading toward Bunk 7.

Ricky stood up. "Guess we'd better get going."

"I'll walk you," Norman said eagerly. She ignored him. Instead, she turned to Steve, batted her eyelashes and waited for him to fall panting at her feet.

"See you," he said mildly. I realized I hadn't breathed for a moment, while I waited to see if he would follow Ricky.

"Come on, Norman," she snapped. She snatched up her blanket and stalked off. Norman trotted beside her, trying to keep up.

"See you, Mel," said Steve, just the way he'd said it to Ricky.

"Steve," I pleaded. But he'd already turned away and I guess he didn't hear me.

I wanted to follow him as he started toward Bunk 8. I should have followed him. I didn't want him to leave like this. We had to talk, to work this out. It was only a little misunderstanding.

But I couldn't. I couldn't chase him, couldn't force myself on him. I had practically begged him to talk on the marshmallow line. If he'd wanted to talk to me he would have. He would have walked me to the bunk. He didn't want to. He didn't want me. He made that perfectly clear.

I plucked my blanket off the grass and clutched it to me. I felt just like I did the first night of camp, when I was homesick. There was that same empty, hollow hunger, but now, along with it, came a dull ache that seemed centered in the pit of my stomach.

Alone, holding a scratchy, gray blanket instead of Steve's hand, I walked back to my bunk.

EIGHT

I stood in center field, the sun beating down on my head, and thought about how unfair life was.

Up until now I would have given anything to have the chance to be on Steve's softball team. I remembered all the days I had spent without so much as a glimpse of him. Now that Steve didn't love me anymore, Uncle Howie, who did the scheduling, suddenly decided the Senior Boys and Girls would enjoy some coed softball.

It was almost impossible for me to keep my mind on the game. I couldn't take my eyes off first base — Steve's position — no matter what was happening around me. I played the first three innings in a daze, aware of very little but a blue and white striped T-shirt that seemed miles away from center field.

A crack of the bat would signal me that something was happening; when I heard that, I would rouse myself enough to try and see where the ball was going. I prayed for a high fly that I would somehow miraculously catch, just to hear Steve shout, "Nice catch,

Mel.'' That would have been enough to make me happy.

But nothing came my way. At least, nothing I could catch.

Finally, in the fourth inning, Jay hit one that soared into the air and started coming down not two feet from where I was standing. I hardly had to move to get under it. It thunked neatly into my glove. Happily, I held it up for everyone to see. I waited to hear Steve call, ''Nice catch, Mel!''

Instead, Duncan screamed, ''Throw it to third, Mel! No, throw it in!''

While I'd been gloating over my catch, a runner on first and a runner at third had tagged up and scored.

Nobody yelled, ''Nice catch, Mel.'' But Ricky clapped and shouted, ''Way to go, outfield!''

She was on the other team.

Dunc, who was pitching, was in a frenzy by the time I shook off my confusion. I threw the ball as hard as I could to second base. It didn't get that far, but by then it didn't matter, since there was no one left on base to put out.

When Duncan calmed down he yelled, ''Pay attention out there, Mel!''

''Okay,'' I said. I was bitterly disappointed that nobody (meaning Steve) recognized what a terrific catch I had just made. *I* was pleased that I had made a catch at all. But I promised myself I'd pay more attention to what was going on and maybe I would make another terrific catch and even hurl the ball to home plate so hard I'd put out a runner trying to score. How I'd suddenly be able to throw a ball that far, when I couldn't even get it to second base, was something I refused to worry about.

''Everybody back! Get back!'' That meant Ricky was up. Every time she came up, Duncan sent the infield into the outfield and the outfield into where the bleachers would have been if we were playing in Yankee Stadium.

Ricky hit the first pitch deep into left field. Audrey let it fall behind her and had to scramble after it. She threw it toward third, but it didn't get there and Norman, who was playing third, raced to scoop it off the grass. He turned and fired toward home as Ricky rounded third base and headed for the plate.

Ricky dropped like a duck in a shooting gallery and crumpled in a heap on the baseline.

For a second there was only shocked silence and then someone shrieked, "You hit her!" and everyone raced toward where Ricky had fallen.

By the time I got there, Anne was kneeling over Ricky and shooing everyone away. Ricky sat up slowly, winced and grabbed at the back of her head. She closed her eyes and grimaced in pain.

Norman looked horrified.

"Just sit there," Anne was saying. "Just sit for a minute."

"Are you all right?" Diane asked. "Ricky, are you all right? Can you get up?"

"Be quiet, Diane!" Anne barked. "Go and get Uncle Howie and if you can't find him, get Uncle Dan."

"But Anne—" she wailed.

"Go!"

She ran off.

In a few minutes, Uncle Dan arrived, running, with Diane on his heels. He and Anne helped Ricky to her feet and toward the main house, where his station wagon was parked. They were going to take her into town for X rays at Milgrim Hospital.

We sat round talking in hushed whispers after they left, just like someone had died. Nobody felt like playing softball anymore. They just wanted to talk about Ricky. Norman was miserable.

"It was my fault," he kept repeating. "I hit her. I never meant to hit her."

No one blamed him and everyone told him that, but it didn't help. He just kept moaning about how it was his fault.

I tried very hard to feel sorry for Ricky. I really did. I knew I ought to feel sorry for her. I tried to imagine how it would feel to get hit in the head with a softball and all I could think of was, "That really must have hurt." I told myself I would never be as brave as she was. She hadn't even cried, and if it were me, I would have been blubbering all over the place.

Of course, that might mean she wasn't that badly hurt after all. If she was knocked unconscious, it must have only been for a couple of seconds. But still, I should feel sorry for her. Well, I did feel sorry for her. I might have felt a lot sorrier for someone else who got hit in the head, but I did feel sorry for her.

Except for Sarah, who was talking quietly with Alan, and Diane, who sat in silent misery, all the other girls, who didn't like Ricky any more than I did, were putting on these long, serious faces, and replaying the whole scene. They were acting very shocked and concerned. I thought they sounded phony. I was sure they were talking this way to impress the boys with how tenderhearted they were. I felt like yelling, "Hypocrites!" at the whole bunch of them.

Steve was standing with Joanie and Harvey. I started over to them. I wouldn't say anything, I'd just listen. I wanted to be next to Steve, even if he didn't say a word to me. I just wanted to feel him standing close to me, close enough so that I might touch the sleeve of his blue and white striped shirt. The part with his biceps in it.

But Steve was walking away. He headed toward the outfield, probably going to his bunk.

I sighed. "Hey, Joanie," I called listlessly, "I'm going back to the bunk, okay?"

Steve turned around. For an instant, he looked in my direction and I froze. *Come back,* I thought fiercely. *Turn around and come back. I love you.* I concentrated like mad, trying to force my thought waves on him.

But the moment was over and we each turned back toward our own bunk.

Ricky had a mild concussion, She was going to spend a few days in the infirmary because she had to rest. Ricky lounged on her cot while Anne gathered up her clothes and things, and Diane tried eagerly to be helpful. Finally Anne told her she could help carry Ricky's stuff to the infirmary and Diane beamed like she had just been presented with an Academy Award.

Everyone took turns asking Ricky how she felt. I had to admit that she looked like she was in pain, but on the other hand, she seemed to enjoy all the attention. She was quiet and soft-spoken to everyone; I was almost ready to believe that the accident had changed her personality, that she had somehow had one of those deathbed experiences that teaches you that life is too short to be wasted picking on people.

And then, just as she was about to leave, with Diane standing there with piles of Ricky's stuff in her arms and Anne holding one of her elbows, she turned to me and said, "Your Steve is so sweet, Mel. Do you know, when I got hit, he was the very first one to run over to me?"

And they left. *Bam,* the door slammed behind them. Hit and run.

My stomach churned. I didn't know what part of Ricky's little tidbit to cry over first. "Your Steve."

Did she know he wasn't *my* Steve anymore? Or did she think he still was and wanted me to be jealous?

Why was he so worried about her? Why was he the first one to run to her?

Sarah sat down next to me on my cot. "She just said that to make you feel bad."

"Is it true?"

"I don't know." She shrugged. "But so what?"

"Oh, Sarah, everything's crummy."

"Mel, I'll bet he's just waiting for you to say something. I think he really feels that you worry more about Dougie than him." We'd talked about this before, and she'd said the same thing.

"I can't. I don't want to chase him. What if he really *doesn't* like me any more? I'd look like an idiot."

"He wouldn't stop liking you that fast," she said. "That's silly. He's not that type anyway. He's just waiting for you to make the first move."

"But he should make the first move. *He* started it. He got mad at *me*."

"Oh, Mel, you're making up these dumb little rules. What difference does it make if you think he started it? Maybe he feels you started it by taking Dougie's side again."

"But why was he the first one to go running to Ricky?"

Sarah threw up her hands in disgust. "Because he's a nice guy. Because he was closest to her. Because he runs fastest. How do I know? And if she was knocked out, how does *she* know? Everyone ran over there. What difference does it make?"

"I don't want to be pushy. Maybe he likes Ricky now instead of me and I don't want to act like she did and make a fool of myself."

"Well," said Sarah, "what if I talk to Alan and have him talk to Steve?"

"What do you mean? What would he say?"

"The same thing you would if you weren't so scared of looking pushy. You know, that it was all a misunderstanding and that you still like him and does he like you?"

"Oh, Sarah, no! That's so obvious!"

"But it's the truth!" Sarah said, exasperated.

"Yeah, I know, but—"

"Maybe Alan could be a little more subtle about it. Sort of feel him out, you know?"

"You think he could? Do it without being too obvious, I mean?"

Sarah regarded me with surprise. "Of course." How could I doubt that Alan could do anything? she seemed to be saying.

"I don't know." I sighed. "I'll think about it."

I must have thought about it for hours that night before I fell asleep. I was feeling so rotten it was hard to think clearly. What if Steve told Alan he didn't like me anymore? What if Alan made it sound as if I was practically dying of a broken heart? Steve would think I was very uncool. *He* wasn't dying of a broken heart, I was sure of that. Then he would think I loved him more than he loved me, and I didn't want him to think that. Even if it was true.

Maybe I would just have to learn to live with that aching emptiness in my midsection. It wasn't getting better. We'd been eating Visiting Day junk food all afternoon and evening, but it hadn't done a thing to fill the hollow space that now seemed to be at the very center of my whole body.

Visiting Day seemed like it had happened a year ago. Everyone was asleep but me, and I never felt so alone in my life.

NINE

My riding lesson was scheduled right after clean-up, which was probably a good thing. This way, I wouldn't have all day to work myself into a frenzy worrying about starting to canter.

On the other hand, I had slept so little the night before that I was tired, and I was still thinking very fuzzily when Sarah asked me if I had made up my mind about asking Alan to talk to Steve.

We were policing the area, which was our job for clean-up. This meant walking around the outside of the bunk in search of litter. I felt tired, depressed and nervous all at the same time and Sarah was insisting that I make a decision.

"Oh, all right, all right," I said finally, "tell Alan to talk to him. But Sarah, please," I added, "for heaven's sake, tell him to be casual about it. Tell him not to make it sound like a big deal."

"Sure, sure," Sarah said. Her eyes sparkled. "Alan will fix everything. Maybe he can just sort of work it into the conversation."

"Sure," I said glumly. " 'And by the way, Steve,

Sarah said that Mel said that I should tell you she's foaming at the mouth to see you again.' ''

Sarah giggled. "I think Alan can be a little more subtle than that."

Right after Uncle Howie came to inspect the bunk I headed for the riding ring. Although I was still depressed, I was beginning to feel a lot more nervous. There's nothing like fear to take your mind off your troubles. No matter how slowly I walked—and I walked pretty slowly—there was no way that I was going to arrive so late that the period would already be over.

Carol, who was an experienced rider, had wished me luck. "You'll love cantering," she said. "The only thing you have to remember is to stick close to the saddle."

"That's just what I'm worried about," I said. "Staying in the saddle."

"Oh, everybody falls off a horse once or twice. As long as you get your feet out of the stirrups you can't get too hurt."

"Gee, thanks, Carol," I said. "That makes me feel a lot better."

I thought of this conversation as I walked past the Arts and Crafts shack. I could see the whole scene: Marlon cantering, me falling, my foot stuck in the stirrup, Marlon still cantering, cheerfully unaware that he was dragging me along the ground to my death.

I was not in the rosiest frame of mind when I reached Karen and Marlon.

In fact, I was so nervous that not only did I forget to be depressed about Steve, but I nearly forgot that I wasn't talking to Karen.

"Let's get going, Mel. You're late."

Not late enough, I thought gloomily. Though an hour from now I might very well be the "late Melanie Kessler."

I walked slowly toward Marlon.

"You did just great Saturday," she said. "I'll bet your parents were proud."

"Yeah, they were."

"You looked so calm and self-confident. Your seat was beautiful."

"Thanks."

"It's hard to believe I'm turning such a scaredy-cat into a real horsewoman. I'm pretty proud of myself."

I whirled around and glared at her. She had her head cocked to one side and a bland little smile on her face.

She's proud of *herself*. *I* nearly drown, *she* does nothing to rescue me and now she calls me a coward. I'd been going to suggest that maybe Marlon needed to be groomed and perhaps today would be a good day to use my lesson time to curry him, but I changed my mind. She might think I was scared to canter.

Yeah, but I am scared to canter, I reminded myself. But Karen doesn't have to know that. I don't have to give her another reason to laugh at me. Scaredy-cat, huh? *I'll show her.*

Without another moment's hesitation I unwrapped Marlon's reins from the rail and practically leaped into the saddle.

"Trot him around a couple of times and then go on out to the field. Keep him trotting. Don't let him slow to a walk."

I trotted twice around the ring. Marlon wanted to stop in front of his place to eat some grass. I didn't let him. I pressed my knees in close and turned him toward the opening in the fence. I kicked him just hard enough to remind him he was supposed to be trotting and headed him out of the ring. Karen strolled after us.

"Keep him trotting," she called. "When you get into the open, lean forward and to your right a little and kick him up so he knows you want him to go faster.''

I don't *want* him to go faster, I thought — but only for a second. I had to pay attention to Karen's instructions.

''Stop posting when he starts to canter. Just stay down in the saddle and keep your knees in and your heels down. You'll get bounced pretty hard a couple of times, but then it'll be nice and smooth if you keep your seat right.''

If I keep my seat at *all*.

The field stretched out for what seemed like miles, although it really wasn't that big. It was such a beautiful morning. The short clipped grass was still damp with dew and the air was crisp and cool. Just a couple of white clouds puffed across the bluest sky . . . It would be a shame to spoil a beautiful day like this by getting killed.

I took a deep breath, stopped posting and leaned forward. I kicked Marlon's flanks and got smacked hard in the backside by the saddle, because Marlon was still trotting. I made clicking noises with my teeth and kicked him again — like I meant business. And all of a sudden Marlon's head went forward and after two more beats of his tame trot his right leg shot out in front of him.

I got three good jolts against the saddle, then felt my seat adjust nice and close as I remembered to keep my knees in . . . and we were flying!

''Keep the reins close,'' Karen yelled. ''Elbows looser. Don't worry about the stirrups. Look straight ahead! Keep him going, keep him going!''

My heart pounded as we raced across the field. Oh, what a beautiful horse! Oh, to feel my hair blowing out behind me! Oh, why couldn't my parents see me now! How gorgeous Marlon and I must look!

I was so excited that I forgot to keep signaling

Marlon and before I knew it he had slowed down to a trot and then a tired, panting walk.

I relaxed and sat back in the saddle, loosening the reins a little. I was panting too. My heart was still pounding and I was grateful to have the opportunity to catch my breath.

I turned Marlon around and walked him slowly back to Karen.

"Fantastic. Beautiful," she raved. "I don't believe it."

"Me neither! Who would have thought old Marlon had it in him?"

"That's not what I meant," she muttered.

Marlon lowered his head to nibble some clover.

"Again," she said. "Start him into a trot and then make him canter. Be firm. He's going to try and pretend he's too tired. I want you to keep him going. Keep your heels in. Don't try to turn him yet. Just go to the end of the field and he'll probably stop by himself the minute you let up on the pressure. If you lose a stirrup, forget about it. Don't look for it."

Again. The same thrill, the same breathtaking sensation of flying, this time all the way to the end of the field. Sure enough, Marlon slowed down by himself. But when I turned him back toward Karen I made him trot back across the field. Two canters and I had turned into a speed freak! I couldn't wait to start again.

"That's it, Mel! You showed him who's boss! Let him walk around for a while now. Keep his head up. Don't let him eat grass."

I walked him. Impatiently. I was eager to be flying. Now that I knew what he and I could do together, walking and trotting seemed as bland as baby cereal.

The period sped by. I couldn't get enough of cantering. Too soon it was time to return to the ring and leave Marlon, wheezing dramatically at the rail.

Karen put her hand on my shoulder. "Mel," she said, "you're a natural-born rider."

"Yeah, I know," I said joyfully. My whole body tingled with excitement. "What comes after cantering?"

I wanted to run back through the woods to the main campus, fling myself into the cabin where they kept the PA system and announce, "MELANIE KESSLER CANTERED TODAY! NOT ONLY THAT, SHE IS A NATURAL-BORN RIDER."

I was really too tired to run, so I just walked, but the spring in my step made me bounce along like I was striding across trampolines.

"Camptown ladies sing this song, doo dah, doo dah . . ." I didn't hum, I sang good and loud. I didn't care who heard me. I hoped *everyone* would hear me. Why not? I can *canter*.

"Camptown racetrack five miles lo—"

I stopped dead in front of the Arts and Crafts shack. There, on his very own rock, in exactly the same position as I had seen him the first time, was Dougie.

I had the eerie feeling that I had been through all this before. Then I reminded myself that there was nothing eerie about it. I *had* been through it before.

"What's the matter, Dougie? How come you're out here again? They're not still making lanyards?"

He jumped off his rock and ran up to me. "Was that you singing, Mel? I heard someone singing."

"That was me. Now, what's the matter? Why aren't you inside?"

He took my arm. "You're a good singer, Mel. You have a good voice."

"Dougie," I said firmly, "I'm glad you like my singing, but why are you out here alone again?"

"Nobody likes me," Dougie sniffled. "Even Joel doesn't like me."

102

"Oh, Dougie, that's not true. I like you. And I'll bet Joel likes you too. Why do you say that?"

"Because it's true. And Celia said I couldn't have any blue paint."

"Hey, wait a minute. I'm getting confused."

When I finally managed to untangle the whole story it was something like: Everybody got to choose one jar of paint to use in painting the clay masks they had made last time. Everybody got the color they wanted except Dougie. Either he didn't move fast enough or he didn't speak up soon enough, but whatever happened, by the time he got to choose all the blue paint was taken. And no one would let him share. No, he didn't want green paint or yellow paint or red paint. His mask had to be *blue*.

And when he insisted that he wouldn't paint his mask any other color but blue, all the kids had called him a spoiled brat and a baby for making such a fuss. When they wouldn't stop picking on him, he just walked out.

"But the period's over, isn't it? Why didn't you go back to your bunk? Joel didn't just leave you here, did he?"

"I told you," he said impatiently. "Nobody likes me. I'm not going back. I hid over there," he pointed toward a tangle of bushes several yards away, "and I didn't make a sound when Joel called me." He sounded almost proud of himself for being such a good hider.

"But you can't sit here the whole rest of the summer," I tried to reason with him. "Look, I have to get back to my own bunk. I'm already late. Why don't we go back together?"

"*No*," said Dougie. "I'm not going back."

"Well, okay then, just walk me to my bunk and we can talk on the way and then you can come back here. Because I can't stay and talk anymore. I'm late."

He hesitated a moment, then slid down off the rock.

I tried very hard to understand what he was feeling but it seemed like an awfully big fuss over a little paint.

"I guess," I began slowly, "you really had your heart set on making that mask blue, huh?"

"Yeah."

"You had it all planned. You had this picture in your mind of a blue mask and you just couldn't see it any other color."

"Yeah." He kicked a pebble out of our path.

"You must have the soul of a true artist," I said.

"I do?" He stopped and looked at me. "What does that mean?"

"You're very artistic. You know how you want things to look. They have to be just right."

"Right," he agreed.

"You know what you want and nobody can talk you out of it."

"Yeah," he said, thrusting out his jaw.

"But how do you get what you want?"

"What?"

"When you knew you wanted blue paint, what did you do to get blue paint?"

"Everybody was pushing and shoving and yelling out colors so I waited till they went back to the tables."

"But then it was too late."

"I don't like to get pushed and shoved," he said, scowling.

"Me neither. But sometimes you have to do some pushing yourself to get what you want. I mean, if that's what everyone else is doing."

"Are you still friends with my brother?" he asked abruptly.

Had he heard a word I said?

"Or is that other girl his girl friend now? He talked to her all the time at the cookout and didn't say anything to you."

Why did he have to bring that up, just when I was feeling so good?

We were approaching the bowl of the main campus now. Forget about Steve. The question is, how am I going to get this kid back to his bunk?

"Well, I don't know, Dougie . . ."

"Would you still be my friend anyway?"

"Of course!"

"Good. I was worried." He looked up at me, his big eyes hopeful and expectant. "Then could you talk to Celia about letting me have blue paint?"

I nearly exploded with frustration. He *hadn't* been listening to me. Here I was trying to use child psychology on him, and thought I was doing pretty well for a beginner with no experience except for watching an expert on a talk show once. And all he was worried about was how to get me to fight his battles for him.

For the first time I think I began to understand Steve's point of view.

I knelt down and grasped Dougie's shoulders so I could look him straight in the eye.

"Listen to me, Dougie. I'm your friend, right?"

"Right!"

"Okay." I took a deep breath. "I'm not going to talk to Celia for you. I can't."

His face crumpled. "But, Mel—"

"Shh! I'm your friend. I'm on your side. But *you* have to be on your side too."

He looked puzzled.

"You don't like it when the kids call you baby. You don't like it when they pick on you. Do you want them to stop?"

He nodded. Then he looked down at his sneakers.

"Don't let them *think* you're a baby. Don't act like a baby."

"I don't," he whined.

"A big boy doesn't ask his brother or his counselor or anyone else to do his fighting for him. A big boy stands up for himself. And if somebody shoves him, he shoves back."

He kept staring at his toes.

"You understand what I mean, don't you, Dougie?"

He nodded slowly, but he didn't look up at me.

"And I'll tell you something else. Friend to friend. You're in a bunk with a lot of other kids. Sometimes you have to do something because everyone has to do it. Like taking Arts and Crafts. Sometimes you have to cooperate. Only babies get their own way all the time."

"But you said I *should* get what I want."

Hmm. I did say that, didn't I? Well, at least he was listening a little.

"When you're entitled to it," I said, after a moment's hesitation. "When it's reasonable. But it's not fair for you to get your own way when nobody else is getting their way. Dougie, I want you to go back to your bunk. Joel is probably worried sick about you. Now — what are you going to do?"

"Cooperate," he mumbled. "Push back."

"Just try, Dougie," I urged, I gave him a quick hug, then stood up and walked him to Bunk 2. He didn't argue. He also didn't say good-bye as he trudged up the steps into his bunk.

I sighed. Then I hurried down the grass slope and past the flagpole in the center. I had given Dougie a great pep talk, but I really didn't think I was going to work any miracles. I wasn't going to change him in five minutes if no one else had been able to change him in seven years. Probably the only thing I'd ac-

106

complished was persuading him not to sit on that rock the whole summer.

But what if I did get through to him? What if he did change? Maybe he didn't listen to Steve because he was so used to hearing criticism from him. Maybe he'd believe me because I was his friend and not his brother.

Wouldn't Steve be pleased! "Melanie, I don't know how you did it but it's a *miracle*. He's a new person! How will I ever be able to thank you?" I would snuggle into the curve of his arm and whisper in his ear, "You'll think of a way."

When I got back to the bunk everyone was gone. I glanced at the schedule near the door and found that I was missing General Swim.

"Oh, what a shame," I giggled to myself. "Oh, darn." I headed straight for the shower.

I was half undressed when it hit me. Steve had been right. I had been wrong. I had just told Dougie exactly what Steve had been telling him—and trying to tell *me*. Steve was angry at me because of Dougie. Which made our whole "misunderstanding" my fault. Which meant I had a perfect reason to go to Steve and tell him the whole story and say I was sorry. And once I said I was sorry, everything would be all right again!

Was anyone ever so happy to have been wrong? Did anyone ever feel this much joy at the thought of having to say "I'm sorry"?

Oh, what a beautiful morning! I learned to canter, cured Dougie, and was about to mend two broken hearts.

And I had the shower all to myself!

TEN

$\mathbf{B}$y the time the others returned I was stretched out on a blanket in the sun,
drying my hair and writing a bubbly letter home.

"And where have *you* been?" Anne demanded.

"I got back late from my lesson," I explained. "I
cantered today."

"That's great!" Anne exclaimed. She ruffled my
damp hair and I smoothed it back down.

"Hey, how'd you do?" Carol asked.

"I was wonderful!" I said. "Karen said I was a
natural-born rider."

"I knew you'd love it!" she said.

Everyone except Diane congratulated me before
they hurried into the bunk to get dressed for lunch.
Diane hadn't said much since Ricky went to the infirmary. She just walked around looking like she had
a dark cloud over her head.

How peaceful it seemed with Ricky gone.

Sarah squatted down on my blanket after everyone
else was inside.

"I didn't get to see Alan yet. I thought I might at

swim, but the boys weren't there. If I hurry, I might be able to talk to him at the mess hall."

"Oh, hey, I forgot all about that."

"Forgot? Mel, how could you forget? You couldn't think of anything else since—"

"Yeah, but listen to what happened." I told her the whole story of my talk with Dougie, almost word for word. And while I heard myself repeat the things I had said to Dougie, I began to feel a little weird.

My voice slowed down almost to a crawl as I listened to myself play back my own advice. I gazed out across the campus at the flag whipping around the flagpole.

A big boy doesn't ask his brother or his counselor to do his fighting for him.

A big boy stands up for himself.

What about a big girl?

Sarah waved her hand in front of my face. "Mel? You still here?"

"Yeah. I was just thinking . . ."

Diane dashed down the bunk steps and took off across campus.

"What's with her?" I asked curiously.

"Anne told her she could visit Ricky in the infirmary before lunch. What were you thinking about?"

"A lot of things," I said vaguely. "But listen, don't tell Alan to talk to Steve. I want to tell him myself how I understand Dougie now."

"Sure, okay," said Sarah. "That's what I thought you should do in the first place, remember? But you didn't want to look pushy."

Sometimes you have to do some pushing yourself to get what you want.

My mind was beginning to act like a tape recorder. It seemed to be going from "rewind" to "play" and back, over and over again—and somehow I couldn't find the "stop" button.

We got to the mess hall before the boys. Anne, Joanie and Diane went right in, but Sarah and I and the others stayed outside and tried to look casual, like we weren't waiting for the boys to show up, even though we were.

We stood a little distance from the steps so we wouldn't be trampled by the other campers, especially the younger ones, who usually thundered into the mess hall like a cavalry charge.

When I saw Steve and Jay coming toward us I sort of detached myself from the other girls. Steve saw me and hesitated. Jay went right over to Carol.

"Hi, Steve," I said softly.

"Hi." He looked puzzled.

"Could I talk to you a minute?"

"Sure." He shrugged as if it didn't matter to him one way or the other. I felt a little chill. It *had* to matter to him, when it meant so much to me.

"I saw Dougie today."

He stiffened. "You want to talk about my brother? Didn't you get enough of him yet?"

"Please listen! Please, Steve, you don't even know what I want to say."

"I'm listening."

"What I wanted to tell you was that when I talked to him today I began to think that you were right and I just didn't understand him very well."

His eyes got wide. Then he frowned and shook his head like he wasn't sure he'd heard right.

"I sort of gave him a lecture about standing on his own two feet and not depending on other people to get him out of things."

"You're kidding."

110

"I'm not kidding. And listen—I'm sorry. I mean, I think I was wrong. And I can see why you were mad at me."

"Ah, Mel," he said, his voice all gentle, "I wasn't mad at you. I was just—"

Uncle Howie practically pounced on us. "Aren't you two planning to eat?" he said heartily. "Come, come, you have to keep your strength up."

I sighed and let him steer us into the mess hall. We didn't even get to hold hands, because Uncle Howie walked between us with his arms draped chummily around our shoulders.

We must have been among the last ones into the mess hall because everyone else was already eating. Steve managed to work his way out from under Uncle Howie's arm and gave my hand a quick squeeze before he sat down. He didn't say anything, but that was okay. He didn't have to.

I practically skipped all the way to our table.

I sat down between Sarah and Carol. There was a plate of something already set at my place.

"Well, what have we here?" I asked.

"What happened, Mel?" asked Sarah. "How'd it go?"

"Oh, isn't this nice!" I said. "Little bits of stuff in cream sauce."

"Mel," Sarah insisted.

I was in a very teasing mood. "And little green things, too. How adorable."

Sarah gave me a swift jab in the ribs. "Melanie Kessler, if you don't answer me—"

Carol was giggling at the whole exchange. "Aunt Ilene said it's Tuna Surprise," she said helpfully. Sarah glared across me at Carol.

"I guess the little green things are the surprise," I said.

"No," said Carol, "I think the surprise is that there's no tuna in it."

"All right," snapped Sarah. "Don't tell me."

"Sarah," I whispered, "look at my face. Do I look like a happy person or an unhappy person?"

Sarah scowled.

"I'll tell you later," I murmured. "Everything's fixed."

I took a bite of my Tuna Surprise. "Bleahh!" Suddenly I sobered up. I pushed the plate away.

"And to think, a tuna died for this."

The next few days were perfectly glorious.

Though I didn't see Steve much except for a few minutes before meals, we had a square dance one night and a movie another, and while I wanted to be with him all the time, I gladly settled for an hour or two at evening activity.

The movie was a full-length cartoon version of *Moby Dick* and was probably dreadful, but with Steve holding my hand and whispering snide comments about it in my ear the whole time, I didn't — as usual — concentrate on it too much. Mostly I remember that the white whale sounded like he had asthma.

When it was over I said, pretending I had watched it, "Uncle Dan's movies are almost as good as his records."

"Better," nodded Steve.

The square dance was held "under the lights," which meant outdoors on the basketball court. The lights were a couple of poles with yellow anti-insect bulbs in them.

"Uncle Dan doesn't waste money on hundred-watt bulbs," Reenie explained.

The lights were hardly bright enough to light up a basketball court, which is why, I suppose, we never actually got to play basketball under the lights. And they didn't do much to distract the bugs, either, because even with such dim lighting they found me with no trouble at all.

Carol had warned me to spray some "Bug-Off" on myself before the dance, but I didn't want to smell like insecticide, so I wore my usual Green Apple cologne. I thought Steve liked it. I know the bugs did. I was practically eaten alive.

Even so, and even though I didn't know the first thing about square dancing, it was fun. Steve knew how, from last year, and Uncle Dan was the caller and explained the steps before we started. Uncle Howie played the music on his accordion. Even Anne and Harvey and Joanie and her boy friend, Phil, from Bunk 5, joined in.

I wasn't the only one who didn't know the steps. Sarah and Alan were in our square and they got just as mixed up as I did, so we did a lot of bumping into each other. Our Grand Right and Left, where the square becomes a circle and the boys go one way and the girls another, till you get back to where you started, turned into such a scrambled mess that we ended up doubled over in hysterics.

"You know what?" said Alan. "I think we have the worst square in the whole dance." He sounded proud of our lousiness.

Anne and Harvey, who did know the steps, and were in our square too, tried to get us straightened out by shouting explanations of Uncle Dan's directions, which *he* had to practically scream so he could be heard over Uncle Howie's accordion. That didn't help at all; we got even more confused.

After the dance was over and we had cake and punch, Steve and I walked back to Bunk 7 slowly, as slowly as we could, holding hands. I was beginning to get more used to being with him, so that my heart wasn't constantly going "flutter, flutter, *thud*," but when we were holding hands, or he had his arm around me, there was a lovely feeling of warmth and security. I was sure this was perfect happiness and I wouldn't ever want anything else.

When we got back to the bunk I could hear by the noise level that almost everyone was already inside. Joanie was standing on the steps with Phil, her arms folded.

"Move it, Mel," she ordered. And then, very deliberately, she turned her back.

Steve pulled me around to the side of the bunk. Before I knew what was happening, he put his hands on my shoulders, bent down and kissed me quickly on the lips.

It was over so fast that I didn't even have time to react, except for my heart to pound extra hard a few times.

"I better go," he said.

I wanted to cry out, "Oh, do you *have* to? Can't you stay here and kiss me some more?"

But what I said was simply, "See you." I think it came out more like a squeak than a husky, movie-star whisper.

All of me tingled as I floated up the steps of the bunk and inside.

My first kiss, I told myself.

Like in a dream, I could almost stand back and watch myself gliding toward my cot, turning neither right nor left, looking at no one, deaf to the hubbub around me.

Lou's sudden shriek did manage to burst through my private haze.

"Hey, Anne! The toilet's stoped up!"

ELEVEN

Ricky came back from the infirmary and picked up where she left off without hardly missing a beat. If I thought getting hit in the head with a softball would change her life, I was wrong.

The whole morning got off to a bad start. My riding lesson was cancelled because Karen had a migraine headache. Then there was swimming instruction.

Were we ready to become Sunfish?

"I'll try if you will," I told Sarah.

"I'll try it if you will," she said to me.

"I'll try it if Mel does," Dougie piped up.

"You can't be a Sunfish," Jason told Dougie. "You're not even a Frog yet."

Aunt Rosalind waited impatiently for us to make a decision.

Two laps of the crawl and one minute of treading water. Suddenly the length of our Frog Pond seemed enormous. I had almost done two laps yesterday, but I tired in the middle of the second lap.

But that wasn't during a test. Maybe if I knew it was a test I'd be able to push myself to finish.

"What do you think?" I asked Sarah.

"I don't know." She looked across the beginners' area. "What do you think?"

Aunt Rosalind groaned. "*I* think that the period will be over by the time you make up your minds. Look, if you don't pass today you can always take the test again. What have you got to lose? It won't be the end of the world if you don't make it on your first try."

"Well," I hesitated. "I will if Sarah does."

"Okay," said Sarah. "If Mel wants to. You can go first, Mel."

"Thanks," I said sourly. "But you can go first."

Aunt Rosalind was ready to explode.

"No, that's okay, I don't mind waiting," Sarah said.

"You can both take the test together," Aunt Rosalind said firmly. "At least we'll save some time that way."

She had us go to the deep end where the water was up to our chests. We left plenty of room between us so we wouldn't bump into each other or get distracted.

"Okay, two laps without stopping. Go!"

I took off, trying to move my arms "like a windmill" as Aunt Rosalind always reminded us. I kept my fingers cupped slightly so I wouldn't splash too much and tried to keep my feet kicking rhythmically. The hardest thing, though, was breathing properly. Breathe in when your head turns to the side, breathe out into the water. I had to concentrate; it still didn't seem to come naturally to me.

By the end of the first lap I was tiring. It was a strain to keep kicking; it was even a strain to keep my legs from sinking down till my feet touched bottom. I hated to open my eyes under water, so I just opened

116

them when my head was up, but they were beginning to sting because the water was constantly dripping into them.

Halfway through the second lap I was out of breath. I hated the water, hated swimming, hated this stupid, unnatural breathing I had to do. By now I could hardly breathe at all. I was panting and I couldn't get enough air in between strokes. Then I made the same dumb mistake I'd made at my first swimming lesson. I breathed in when my head was under water. I couldn't help it. I was panting too hard to stop myself.

The water rushed up my nose and down my throat. I began to sputter and choke; the back of my throat felt raw. I stood up right away. As soon as my feet touched bottom I failed the test, but all I cared about was getting the water out of my nose.

I wiped my eyes just in time to see Sarah reach the end of her second lap and bob up joyfully, both hands raised over her head. The whole group cheered and applauded.

"Good girl!" Aunt Rosalind cried. "Nice try, Melanie, You almost made it. You'll pass next time."

What next time? I waded back to the shallow water as Aunt Rosalind started timing Sarah treading water.

I was still coughing.

"Too bad you didn't pass, Mel," said Dougie sympathetically. "But I'm glad you're staying in my group."

"Yeah." Lucky me, I thought. Now I was the only Senior who was still a Frog. Sarah finished treading water and Aunt Rosalind and everyone else was clapping. I clapped too. I wanted to feel happy for Sarah, I wanted to be able to congratulate her, but I was feeling too sorry for myself to be very sincere about it.

I'd been right in the first place. Some of us were

not cut out to be the Big Fish. I might as well face it. I'd just have to settle for being the biggest Frog in the pond.

So when we got back to the bunk after swimming and found Ricky sprawled on her cot reading *Mad* magazine, I figured that was about what you'd expect, considering the way the day had gone so far.

"How are you feeling?" I asked politely. Everyone else was being nice to her, and I guess some of them really meant it. After all, no one had as much reason to hate her as I did.

"Oh, pretty good. It was kind of boring in the infirmary, though."

Maybe if you learned to read something besides comic books you wouldn't have been so bored, I thought. But I didn't say it.

"If it wasn't for Steve I would've gone nuts."

The whole bunk was suddenly quiet. Audrey's eyelash curler stopped halfway to her face. Reenie seemed frozen with one foot out of her wet bathing suit bottom. Everyone was looking at me.

"We really had fun when he came to visit."

I felt sick. For a moment I thought my heart had stopped beating. What was she talking about? How had Steve kept her from going nuts? He'd been with me all week — at least, he'd been with me for evening activity. But during the day I had only seen him before meals, so how did I know how he'd spent all those other hours?

But he loved me! He'd never said it, but he'd kissed me and that was the same as saying you loved someone.

Everybody was waiting for me to react. Finally, I muttered, "Yeah, he's very thoughtful," and fled into the bathroom.

Sarah came after me. I just leaned against the cubbies, letting my wet bathing suit turn clammy, trying not to cry.

"What a crock," Sarah said angrily.

"How could he do that?" I moaned, "I really thought he liked me."

"She's a liar, that's all. You ask Steve."

"I can't! I'm not going to check up on him."

"You're not checking up on him, you're checking up on *her*."

"If he wanted to tell me he was seeing her behind my back, he would have told me!" That didn't make much sense, but I wasn't in any condition to make sense.

"He didn't tell you because it didn't happen," Sarah insisted. "And if you don't ask him, I swear I'll ask Alan. I don't know why you take this crap from her. Why do you let her get to you?"

Joanie emerged from the shower. She looked at me and sighed.

"Is she at it again?"

"It's not her, it's Steve," I whimpered.

"It is her," Sarah said. "She really loves to get on Mel. I don't know why Anne doesn't do something."

Joan looked uncomfortable. I wondered why for a moment and then remembered when we had been in the bathroom before and Joan had promised to talk to Anne about Ricky.

I looked over at Joan. Why *hadn't* Anne done anything? I wondered. Why did she and Joan let Ricky go on hassling me all these weeks? Not that it seemed very important now. How Steve felt about me was all that mattered. What did I care if Ricky liked me or hated me? She couldn't make my life any more miserable than it would be if Steve stopped loving me.

Joan dried off quickly, wrapped her towel around her and left the bathroom. Lou and Audrey came in a moment later.

"What did she mean, Mel?" Audrey demanded. I couldn't answer.

"She's lying," Sarah said sharply. "She's just trying to—"

"She's not lying," Diane said. She went into one of the toilets and slammed the door. "I was there. He did visit her."

Sarah pulled me toward the shower. "You get dressed fast," she whispered, "and let's get to the mess hall. We're going to get this cleared up right now."

Dully, I followed orders. Sarah was really furious. I'd never seen her so mad. I was the one who ought to be angry, but Sarah was doing all the carrying-on.

I was in no hurry to get to the mess hall. Sarah practically had to drag me.

"I don't want to talk to him," I said. "Not about Ricky. I'll just pretend nothing happened."

"No you won't," said Sarah. "Maybe you're not sick of Ricky's garbage, but I am. And if you won't do something about it, then I will. And the first thing I'm going to do is prove that it's garbage."

"What are *you* so mad about?" I asked curiously.

She stopped just in front of the mess hall and nearly stamped her foot. "Because you're my friend and I don't like to see you hurt. But you keep letting yourself get hurt. And I can't take it anymore, that's all. Somebody's got to stick up for you and Anne won't do it, and *you* won't do it so—"

She stopped right in the middle of her ranting. A funny look crossed her face. She frowned.

I suddenly felt a little nudge in my brain. Something clicked, and I was just on the verge of making a connection. It was something very important, I knew that. Something important enough to push through, even though I was so miserable I didn't want to think at all.

"There he is," Sarah said, interrupting whatever it was that I was about to figure out. "Now, go ahead."

I hung back. We were so early that there weren't many people around yet and Steve saw me right away. His eyes brightened and he came over to me.

"Hi!" he said, reaching for my hand. Like magic, Sarah disappeared.

"Hi."

"Hey, what's the matter?"

"I—I didn't make Sunfish," I blurted out.

"Aw, that's too bad. But you're okay for a Frog." He smiled down at me and squeezed my hand.

How could he act like this? How could he be so two-faced? Why would he say things like I was "okay for a Frog" when he'd been "cheering up" Ricky the whole week while I thought he loved me?

I couldn't stand it. It was worse not knowing. Maybe I would sound pushy, maybe it was none of my business, but I had to find out.

"You didn't tell me you saw Ricky in the infirmary," I said, the words just spilling out.

He shrugged. "What's to tell?"

"Well, I mean, you didn't even mention it."

"I just brought her a transistor so she could listen to the Red Sox games."

A transistor? But Ricky had her own radio. She took it to the infirmary with her. I saw Diane carrying it.

"Diane went to see her and Ricky said she wished she had a radio and Diane asked me if I had a radio to lend her. That's all."

"How did Diane know you had a radio?"

121

"Maybe Norman told Ricky. He saw her practically every day."

How come he didn't see her radio? Aha! She must have hidden it somewhere. Why didn't she just ask Norman to ask Steve for the radio? Because then she wouldn't have Steve bringing it in person. The whole thing was a *plot*. And Steve didn't realize it. Either that or he didn't care.

"Did you visit her a lot?" I asked casually.

He grinned. "Are you jealous?" He sounded delighted at the idea.

"No, I'm not jealous," I said. "I'm just curious."

"Just curious, huh? You *are* jealous!"

His eyes sparkled. He was really enjoying this.

I snatched my hand from his and turned my back on him pretending to be angry, but it was hard. I knew everything was all right now; that the only reason he hadn't mentioned visiting Ricky was because it was so unimportant to him that he never thought of bringing it up. But I still wanted to know how many times he went to see her.

He turned me around to face him. He held up his index finger. "Once," he said solemnly. "To bring her the radio." He put his finger on my nose. "I like it when you're jealous," he smiled.

"Yeah, I'll bet you do," I grumbled. I swatted his finger away, but I was still only pretending and he knew it.

I couldn't get over it. So much misery cleared up in such a short time! Sarah was right. And even if Ricky hadn't exactly lied, she sure hadn't told the whole truth.

"Hey, do you think you could ask Ricky to give me back my radio when she gets out of the infirmary? All week I've heard nothing but Yankee games. Duncan has the only other radio and unless the Yankees play the Red Sox I don't get to hear a Boston game.''

He was a Red Sox fan too, yet he didn't go to the infirmary except that once, the whole week, even though he could have listened to the games with Ricky!

And he didn't even know Ricky was out of the infirmary!

"Sure," I said, "I'll get it to you." The mess hall was starting to fill up, so we went inside.

"See you later," Steve said. "Don't be sad about being a Frog."

"Wha—oh!" I'd nearly forgotten that I was a Frog. I felt so much like a beautiful princess.

Everybody was at the table when I got there.

Anne said, "Mel, do you think you could get here on time once in a while?"

"*I'm* on time. You're all early."

"I don't understand it," she muttered good-naturedly. "You're the first one out of the bunk and the last one to get to the table. It's very mysterious."

Everyone was watching me expectantly. They could see I was in a good mood and the only people who weren't pleased by it were Ricky and Diane. I thought of the Wicked Witch and her little flying monkey in *The Wizard of Oz*. I nearly burst out laughing.

I choked down the laughter and cleared my throat. "What's Aunt Ilene got for us today?" I asked.

"Chicken Surprise," said Audrey grimly.

"Oh, God, you're kidding." I lost some of my high spirits. "How original. You don't suppose it's anything like Tuna Surprise, do you?"

Our waiter, Ken, started passing down the plates.

"That's the surprise," Carol said, making a horrible face. "It *is* the Tuna Surprise. The *same* Tuna Surprise."

"No it isn't," said Lou. "It's got red things instead of green things. And there's Chinese noodles sprinkled on top."

"Yeah," said Reenie miserably. "Three."

I knew Sarah could hardly stand the suspense. I felt braver than ever, now that I was sure of how Steve felt about me. My, it was amazing what love could do to stiffen the old upper lip!

"Ricky," I began sweetly. Forks stopped. Conversation stopped. It was just like before, in the bunk, but this time it wouldn't end the same way.

"Steve wants to know if he can have his radio back now. He hasn't been able to hear a Red Sox game all week, and now that you're out of the infirmary and don't need it anymore . . ."

Everyone looked mystified.

"But you have a radio, Ricky," Audrey said finally.

Ricky just shoveled in Chicken Surprise like she had a cast-iron stomach.

"Yeah, that's right," said Lou. "And you took it to the infirmary. How come you wanted Steve's radio, Ricky?"

Long silence. Everyone watched Ricky waiting for her to think up a good answer. Finally she muttered, "Batteries wore out."

Audrey giggled. She nudged Reenie with her elbow and Reenie giggled.

Ricky looked up from her plate and glared at them. "You don't believe me?" she asked, daring them not to.

"Sure we believe you," said Reenie. She giggled again.

"Anyway," I cut in, "he asked me to get it back to him, so—"

"I'll give it back," Ricky said irritably.

I was satisfied. But Sarah wasn't.

As the others went back to cursing the Chicken Surprise, Sarah asked, "What really happened? I don't understand any of this."

So I told her.

Carol leaned over to listen. And by the time we got back to the bunk after lunch, everybody had heard what really happened.

Ricky was quiet during rest period. She just lay on her cot and listened to the ball game — on her own radio. I was hoping someone would ask her when she got the batteries, since she only got out of the infirmary that morning, but nobody did. I'm sure everyone noticed it, but that was as far as it went.

Toward the end of rest hour Ricky walked into the bathroom and came out carrying her razor. She started to walk past my cot, then stopped and looked down at me. She "tsk-tsked" exaggeratedly and said, "Why don't you do Steve a favor and use this on your legs?" She dropped the razor at the foot of my cot.

Without thinking, without even realizing what I was going to say, I leaped up and grabbed the razor, I had never felt such blind rage before, but I put the razor back carefully into her hand and my voice sounded almost calm.

"Why don't you do *everyone* a favor," I said, "and use it on your throat?"

And Sarah, very quietly, began to clap.

Ricky stood there, almost as if she were paralyzed.

Now Reenie, then Lou — suddenly all the girls, except for Diane and Ricky, were applauding. Anne looked a little grim, but Joanie was not even trying to hold back a delighted smile.

And just like that, I realized what had been on the

edge of my mind before, the thought that didn't quite come out when I was speaking to Sarah before meeting Steve.

A big boy stands up for himself. A big boy doesn't ask anyone else to fight his battles for him.

That's why Anne didn't tell Ricky to stop picking on me. She was waiting for me to do it. I wasn't a helpless two-year-old baby. I didn't need my counselor, or my friends, or my mother and father to fight my battles for me. Ricky was my battle and it was up to *me* to stick up for *me*.

If somebody shoves you, shove back.

Ricky looked around the bunk, her eyes dark with anger. She opened her mouth to say something as the clapping stopped. But she changed her mind. She charged toward the door, yanked it open and hurtled down the steps.

All I could think of was, *now*. I'm going to take care of her *right now*. My heart pounded and my brain was fired with determination. I flew out of the bunk and down the steps in time to see her stalking around the side of the cabin toward the clothesline in the back.

I caught up with her and without even giving a minute's thought to what I was going to say, plunged right in.

"Look, Ricky, you've been on my back the whole summer and I'm not going to take it anymore."

"You're so brave all of a sudden," she sneered. "Now that you've turned the whole bunk against me."

That stopped me for a moment. Was that why I was suddenly facing up to her? Because I knew almost everyone would be on my side?

I was too charged up to worry about it for more than a second. I didn't care why I was doing it now, I just knew that, at last, I was doing it.

"I didn't turn the whole bunk against you," I said. "You did that yourself. You didn't need any help from me."

"You make me sick," she said. "You really make me sick." Her voice was so full of disgust it shocked me. I stepped back, as if the force of her hatred was strong enough to shove me away.

"You're such a marshmallow," she snarled. "You talk about me behind my back but you haven't got the guts to say anything to my face."

"What?"

"You don't remember saying I'd flunk a hormone test? You don't remember saying I was macho?"

"Oh, for pete's sake, I was angry. You knocked me halfway across the basketball court, you and your little stooge were always screaming about me every time we played a game — you don't remember that? You don't remember all the names you called me?"

"And you never said a thing. The whole time. You were too much of a coward to do anything but talk behind my back. Now all of a sudden, you're brave. Big, brave Melanie."

She turned her back on me.

I didn't feel brave. In fact, I was trembling. If this was going to be my moment of triumph I wasn't enjoying it at all. I didn't like what she was saying to me and I really didn't want to hear any more. I was sorry I had started the whole thing. *I* was beginning to feel a little sick to my stomach. Maybe I wasn't cut out to be a fighter any more than I was cut out to be a swimmer. I wanted to be strong but I felt very little and weak.

But I couldn't just walk away now. I couldn't give up, couldn't give in, couldn't go back to being a marshmallow. That would mean that all the rotten things she said about me were true and the only thing worse than hearing her call me names would be knowing she was right.

I clenched my fingers into fists, as if I were preparing to slug her. I made a real effort to keep my voice from quivering.

"Look, Ricky, I don't care what you think of me. We're never going to be friends so we don't have to pretend we like each other."

She made a choking sound as if the idea of our being friends was enough to make her gag.

"Yeah, I know," I said. "I feel the same way about you. So we'll just agree not to get along with each other. The summer's practically over anyway, so just stay out of my way from now on and I'll stay out of yours. All right?"

I took a deep breath. I had said it. I had done it. Now, what would happen?

She didn't say a word. Her back was rigid. She wasn't going to turn around and look at me.

"All right," I said, just as if she'd agreed. "Fine."

The bugle call sounded the end of rest period. I was grateful that I didn't have time to say anything more, even if I wanted to. I hurried back into the bunk, leaving her still standing there, ramrod straight, looking off into the woods.

TWELVE

Now the morning air was really nippy and we needed sweat shirts when we went to breakfast. When the sun went down in the evenings it was actually cold.

The last week of camp.

I couldn't believe it. I would wake up thinking, "Only seven more days of camp." "Only five more days of camp." Until, the day before we were going home: "The last day of camp."

Never had time raced by so quickly. And the nearer we came to going home, the more speeded up the hours seemed to be, like a movie run too fast, with everybody walking jerkily and doing things in double time.

On the next to the last day of camp I became a Sunfish and Aunt Rosalind passed out little felt badges to all the swimmers. Mine looked like a flat gold fish with SUNFISH lettered on it. Dougie's was a bright green frog. He had made it at last.

I took Marlon for a final canter in the field. I'd learned to turn him without having to slow down. Karen had to practically drag me off Marlon's back at the end of the period. I brought some sugar cubes for him, which I'd filched from the mess hall, and he nuzzled the palm of my hand as he ate them. I told myself he was kissing me good-bye, even though I knew he really wasn't.

Every evening when I saw Steve we were reminded that we had one day less to be together. We began to make elaborate plans to see each other during vacations. He would come to New York, or I would visit him in Connecticut. He'd already written to his mother about inviting me over the Christmas holidays. And we would write to each other, even though he said he wasn't a very good letter writer.

After my showdown with Ricky I had worried that she would pick on me more than ever because of what happened. But she didn't. She hardly talked to me at all at first, except in cold, polite tones, as if to show me how careful she was being not to insult me. But she soon got tired of the act and went back to being almost normal. Only, she was a little quieter and she didn't make one snide remark to me from then on.

The last day of camp was spent almost entirely in packing, exchanging addresses and getting ready for the evening's Awards Banquet. We were going to get dressed up. Everybody had been told to bring one good outfit along, just for tonight. Mine was a soft, silky white dress with little yellow and green flowers all over it. Lou took one look at me in it and said, "Oh, Mel, that's such a *sweet* dress!"

Lou's dress was dark red, with little puff sleeves and a nice, low neck. The hem just grazed the top of her black patent leather sandals.

"Boy," I said, my eyes wide, "yours isn't." I looked from Lou to Audrey, who also had a long dress, and who looked very sophisticated. I looked down at myself. "You know," I said, "I liked this dress a lot better before I saw yours."

"You look beautiful," Audrey said. "Steve will love it."

The mess hall was completely rearranged for the banquet. The tables were set end to end to make an enormous "U" shape that went around the whole hall. At the head table were Uncle Dan and Aunt Ilene, Uncle Howie, Aunt Rosalind and the other specialty counselors who didn't have their own bunks.

There were white tablecloths and napkins and paper flowers everywhere.

"You mean Uncle Dan actually spent all this money for one night?" I asked Reenie.

"Well, we do it every year," Reenie said, "so he could have had the tablecloths for twenty years for all we know. I recognize the flowers, though. He's used the same flowers for the past three years, I'm sure of that."

"But they're only tissue-paper carnations," I said.

"Uncle Dan recycles everything," said Carol.

We had to sit with our own group, but the Senior Boys had gotten there early and kept one whole side of the table opposite them saved for us. When we arrived, there was a bit of a scramble and before Anne or Harvey could say anything, we were all arranged in couples. It happened so fast I'm still not sure how we did it, but the Senior Boys and Girls filled up two tables and as Lou pointed out to Anne, we were still technically with our own groups.

Diane wasn't going with anyone, but she ended up sitting next to a boy named Richard, who wasn't going with anyone either. For the first time I felt a little sorry for her. I thought she was one person who would be glad that camp was over and she could go home.

Steve and I held hands under the table for a while, but I couldn't eat with my left hand too well, so when he saw me struggling to cut my meat he let go.

I loved Steve and I would rather hold hands with him than eat almost any time, but there was roast beef for the banquet, and I think Steve wanted to be able to eat even more than I did.

"Roast beef," I sighed. "I can't believe it."

"Don't get excited, Mel," Reenie called. "He buys it all year whenever it's on special and freezes it. The first thing the little kids will tell their parents when they get home is that they ate roast beef last night. This is supposed to make you forget about all of Aunt Ilene's 'surprises.' "

"It's working," said Sarah. She cut into a roast potato. "I don't care if this is government surplus, it's *great*."

After a dessert of sherbet and cake the waiters cleared the tables and Uncle Dan stood up to start announcing the awards. There were awards for all kinds of things — best swimmer, best athlete (Ricky got that; I clapped as loudly as anyone else). Then there were archery awards, tennis awards, all kinds of awards for achievement in different sports.

After that came the "Most Improved's." Audrey explained what that meant.

"It's when you start out rotten and get one percent better," she said. "Like for Most Improved Camper, it's the kid who started out as the biggest problem and learned to adjust a little after a while."

"Most Improved Camper," announced Uncle Dan, "Douglas Tepper."

Steve looked stunned. Audrey looked like she wanted to crawl under the table. I just screamed and cheered and clapped till my hands and throat were sore.

I did it! I did it! I cured him! I turned Dougie's

whole life around! I ought to be a psychologist, I decided. I was a natural-born psychologist.

I turned to Steve, my face glowing. Now was the time he was supposed to take me in his arms and murmur, "Melanie, I don't know how you did it, but it's a *miracle*. How will I ever be able to thank you?"

But he just kept shaking his head and repeating, "I don't believe it, I don't *believe* it."

Oh well, I didn't really want any thanks for what I had done. It was enough to know I had done it; and besides, love beats gratitude any day of the week.

The next thing I knew, our whole table was yelling and cheering and Sarah was shaking me.

"Mel, you won! Go up there!"

"Me? Me?" I was dazed. "What did I win?"

"Most Improved Rider!"

I leaped up with a shriek and nearly killed myself climbing out over the bench we sat on. I got a quick glimpse of Audrey holding her head in her hands and heard her say something about how she had a big mouth.

My heart was soaring almost the way it did when I cantered for the first time. Karen handed me the award, which was a wooden plaque painted in the camp colors, blue, with white lettering: MOST IM-PROVED RIDER: MELANIE KESSLER.

She kissed me on the cheek. "Congratulations, Mel. You keep up your riding."

I practically ran back to the table. I handed around the plaque so everyone could admire it. Steve gave me a little kiss on the cheek, right in front of everyone. He didn't even seem to mind when they all clapped and laughed.

Anne and Joanie made a big fuss over my award, and then, when Diane got "Most Improved Swimmer," they went a little crazy.

"Three awards in our bunk!" Anne bragged. She passed Diane's plaque to Harvey. "Look at that, Harvey. Three awards for my girls."

Diane smiled. And when Anne said, "Including the best athlete in camp," Ricky beamed. She actually seemed a little bit human then.

Anne, I decided, was a very good counselor.

Steve held my hand so tightly it almost hurt. After he kissed me, he just wouldn't let go of my hand.

Then it was over.

As we came out of the mess hall I saw Dougie with his bunkmates all gathered around him passing his plaque back and forth and making a big deal over it. He looked up and saw us and waved wildly. He snatched the plaque out of Jason's hand and ran over to us.

"Mel, look. Steve, look at my award!"

I read the words on the plaque out loud, with Steve admiring it over my shoulder. " 'MOST IMPROVED CAMPER: DOUGLAS TEPPER.' Boy, Dougie," I said, "are your parents going to be proud of you."

"Yeah!"

Steve patted him on the shoulder. "That's really great, Doug. That's a very big award."

I handed him back his plaque and he clasped it to his chest. Suddenly he looked sad. "I'll miss you, Mel."

"I'll miss you too, Dougie." I knelt down to give him a hug. He threw his arms around my neck and squeezed so hard he nearly strangled me.

"You're my friend," he whispered.

"You bet I am," I whispered back.

"I love you," he said, his mouth right next to my ear.

I kissed his cheek. "I love you too."

He let go of me and stood back a little.

"Mel might come to visit us, Doug," said Steve.

"You will!" Dougie shrieked. "When?"

"Maybe Christmas vacation."

Dougie jumped up and down a couple of times, his whole body alive with excitement.

"And I'll write to you," I promised. "Okay?"

"Okay!" His face was bright again. "And you can write in script," he said. "I can read script."

"I'm sure you can," I laughed.

Holding his plaque high over his head, like he was carrying the Olympic Torch, Dougie ran back to join his group.

We walked back to Bunk 7 in clusters. I was shivering with cold and Steve took off his bulky blue and gray sweater, which, over a blue striped shirt and blue pants, was his dress-up outft. He tucked the sweater around my shoulders. He put his arm tightly around my waist, hugging me to him, so we bumped hips as we walked.

I sighed, thinking that I didn't want this evening to ever end.

"Will you write to me?" he asked.

"Of course. I told you I would. If you write to me."

"I will. But I'm not very good at writing letters."

"I know. You told me."

"But I'll write if you do," he promised.

"I will. You write first, okay?"

"Couldn't you write first?"

Suddenly I felt shy all over again. "Isn't the boy supposed to write first?"

He leaned against the bunk. "Why?"

"I don't know. I just thought he was."

"I didn't know that. I don't think that matters."

I giggled. It was such a silly discussion to waste our precious last minutes on. Thinking about that made me stop giggling right away.

"Okay, I'll write first," I said.

He put his arms around me. "I'll miss you, Mel."

"I'll miss *you*."

I really would. I'd miss everything about camp, but I was sure I'd miss Steve the most. It felt so warm and cozy in his sweater, in his arms.

"I can probably get to New York over Thanksgiving," he said.

"That would be great. Only a couple of months."

"Three," he reminded me gloomily.

"Well, look how fast the summer went," I said.

"Yeah. Too fast."

He kissed me and I hugged him tightly, never wanting to let go. Harvey came down and started rounding up all the boys, who were staying as long as they could at Bunk 7. Steve kissed me again, a beautiful, sad, good-bye kiss. He promised to see me when our bus left in the morning. His parents would be coming to drive him and Dougie home.

I clung to Steve as long as I could, until Harvey practically dragged us apart. "I already gave you guys fifteen minutes extra," he said, over Steve's protests.

I reluctantly took off Steve's sweater and gave it back to him. He handed me my plaque, which he'd been keeping in the sweater pocket for me.

We didn't say anything else. I didn't want to watch him walk away so I went right into the bunk.

It was a madhouse. Most of the girls had come in just before I did and seemed to be in as much of a daze as I was. Our trunks were nine-tenths packed, only last-minute things left to be crammed in. But they were all open and you could hardly move around in the bunk. It was a shambles. Anne and Joan kept barking out orders, but no one was listening. What we were doing mostly was crying.

Diane and Ricky were in great shape, but the rest of us moved around like zombies. I took off my dress — Steve had said I looked pretty — and folded it up. I dropped it into my trunk on top of everything else.

Anne gave up and went into the bathroom to clear out her cubby. I took one look at Sarah, who just sat on her bed looking depressed, and sank down on my own cot.

"I'll miss you, Sarah."

"Me too, Mel."

"You're a good friend."

"You are too. You're the best friend I ever had."

"Aw, come on," I said, sniffling. I put my arms around her and we hugged. "Will you come back next year?"

"If we can afford it, or if they give me a scholarship. I don't know if Alan will, though. Will you?"

"If I can. Remember how homesick we were?"

"Yeah. I feel homesick right now." Sarah laughed. "But you know what? I feel homesick for camp. *Campsick*. Isn't that silly?"

"Maybe. But I know just what you mean."

I did, too. I went into the bathroom and there was Anne, standing in front of all the little cubbies and shaking her head.

"What a mess," she said. "You girls had better get moving."

I sniffled again.

"It's kind of sad, isn't it?" she agreed. "I'm going to miss you all so much."

"Even Ricky?" I whispered, looking around carefully first.

"Even her," grinned Anne.

The tears started down my cheeks, uncontrolled now. I didn't even try to stop them. I needed a good cry. Camp Timberwood had turned out to be my second home after all, and I was going to miss it and my second "family" like crazy.

"Your parents are going to be so proud of you," Anne said.

"My award, you mean?"

"Not just your award. I think your first summer away from home was a big success, don't you?"

"I had a wonderful time," I said, not sure of what she meant.

"I did too," she said. "I enjoyed being your counselor."

I hugged her and started to cry harder. "What'll I do," I sniffed, trying to make a joke, "without you to order me around all the time?"

"You'll manage, Mel," she chuckled, "You'll manage just fine."

I let go of her and wiped my eyes with a towel.

"I'll be okay now," I said.

"I'm sure you will." She grinned.

I smiled back, through a few tears that were still left, and went to finish packing my trunk.

ABOUT THE AUTHOR

ELLEN CONFORD has written many books for young adults, including ANYTHING FOR A FRIEND, and THE THINGS I DID FOR LOVE, coming from Bantam Books in September 1987. HAIL, HAIL CAMP TIMBERWOOD received the California Young Readers Medal. Mrs. Conford is a championship-level Scrabble player and competes in crossword puzzle tournaments. She and her husband live in Great Neck, New York.